## Rachel stared up at him, her breathing ragged

Nick was moving against her, and she had lifted her arms around his neck, surrendering to his kiss. She'd never known anything like this. Guilt stabbed at her suddenly and she drew back horrified. What was she doing?

Drawing a deep steadying breath, she said brightly, "By the way, how much do I owe you?"

He lifted an eyebrow. "Well, that's the first time anyone ever offered to pay me," he taunted, deliberately provocative.

"I meant for fixing the wiring," she enunciated in glacial tones. "Aren't you the electrician?"

"No," he said, his voice ripe with amusement. "I'm moving in upstairs."

"Into the penthouse?"

He nodded. "One of my companies owns this block."

**SUSANNE McCARTHY** has spent most of her life in London, but after her marriage she and her husband moved to Shropshire. The author is now an enthusiastic advocate of this unspoiled part of England, and although she has set her novels in other locations, Susanne says that the English countryside may feature in many of her books.

## Books by Susanne McCarthy

HARLEQUIN PRESENTS

Don't miss any of our special offers. Write to us at the following address for information on our newest releases.

Harlequin Reader Service
P.O. Box 1397, Buffalo, NY 14240
Canadian address: P.O. Box 603,
Fort Erie, Ont. L2A 5X3

# SUSANNE McCARTHY

## a casual affair

*Harlequin Books*

TORONTO • NEW YORK • LONDON
AMSTERDAM • PARIS • SYDNEY • HAMBURG
STOCKHOLM • ATHENS • TOKYO • MILAN

Harlequin Presents first edition November 1991
ISBN 0-373-11412-5

Original hardcover edition published in 1990
by Mills & Boon Limited

A CASUAL AFFAIR

# CHAPTER ONE

'RACHE, I'm sorry...'

'I'm sorry too, Simon.' Rachel pulled the diamond ring from her finger and put it into his hand. 'Here—you'd better have this back.'

He stared at her in disbelief. 'You can't mean this, Rache,' he protested.

'I'm afraid I do,' she asserted resolutely, pride lifting her head. 'Now, if you'll excuse me, I have a programme to record.'

She turned and walked out of his office, holding herself very erect. This had to be a dream—it couldn't be happening. Such a short time ago, everything had been perfect—and then she had overheard something she hadn't been meant to overhear, and suddenly her whole world had been turned upside-down. And with just three weeks to go to the wedding.

One or two people glanced at her strangely as she walked briskly down the corridor. Did they all know? Was she the last one to find out? Some dumb little production assistant from Light Entertainment—she wasn't even *pretty*...

But Rachel wouldn't let her feelings show— she couldn't let them show. In a few moments she had to go before the cameras, and not the faintest shadow of her private distress could be allowed to mar that immaculately packaged public persona. Pinning her coolest professional smile in place, she pushed open the heavy sound-proofed doors of the 'small' studio.

The vast space had a familiar air-conditioned neutrality of smell and temperature. Somewhere on the far side a pool of light bathed a rehearsal that was taking place within the cardboard walls of a South American prison cell. Stepping carefully over the plastic ramp that covered the thick cables snaking across the floor, silent in her soft-soled shoes, she crossed to the set of *In Review*.

It had already been dressed—an elegant Japanese flower arrangement on a low table, a black leather executive-style chair against a simple background of pale matt paper. She was taping only the links this morning—the rest of the programme was already in the can: a good visual piece on the Royal Academy Exhibition, an interview with this year's Booker Prize winner—and Paul, the programme's roving researcher, had sent over his piece from Florence about new developments in the preservation of frescos. A well-balanced package. It would be going out in the late-night slot on Wednesday—the time considered by the experts to be the most suitable for a sophisticated arts review.

'Ready in five, Rachel,' the floor manager warned her.

'Thank you.'

She took her seat in front of the camera, and glanced briefly down at the monitor. The face that gazed back at her was flawless—large, well-spaced hazel eyes, a straight, delicate nose, a soft, slightly sensual mouth, and glossy ash-blonde hair that was easy to arrange in a dozen elegant styles. And the body that went with it all was just as good—tall and very slender, but with curves in all the right places.

It was a beauty she knew that most women would envy, but it had never been a blessing—it had always set her apart. Ever since her early teens, when she had escaped the gawkiness and adolescent spots that her peers were suffering, she had been aware of the jealous hostility of the other girls, the stumbling awe of the boys.

Those years had been miserable. Moving frequently from one school to another as her father's business had prospered and her parents had climbed the social ladder, she had never had a chance to make friends, and her natural shyness had often been misconstrued as stand-offishness.

Until she had met Simon, it had always been the same. Oh, she couldn't help but be aware that men admired her, but it had seemed as if it were the kind of detached admiration they might feel for a fine work of art. They seemed almost afraid to ask her out—maybe it was the cool, sophisticated image of her television career that scared them off. Only Simon had had the assurance to break through her shell. And that made his betrayal so much harder to bear...

'You're frowning, Rachel,' the make-up girl reminded her, coming forward with her box of tricks. 'You'll crease your foundation.'

'Oh...sorry.' She managed a fleeting smile. 'I've got a bit of a headache.'

'Would you like an aspirin?'

'No, I'll be all right in a minute, thanks. A few deep-breathing exercises, that's all.' The merciless glare of the television lights was picking up the tiny lines of tension around her mouth, and consciously she made an effort to relax.

'I love that shade,' the girl went on, admiring the chic burgundy-red silk suit that Rachel was wearing for recording. 'It's really your colour.'

'Thank you.' The girl's last-minute attentions to her face were really hardly necessary, but the calm reassurance was a balm to her bruised nerves.

'Two minutes,' the floor manager warned.

'Oh—you've forgotten your engagement ring,' the make-up girl pointed out, sharp-eyed.

Rachel felt a thud of panic, suppressing the instinct to hide her hand in the folds of her skirt. 'Oh, yes. I...I must have left it in my dressing-room. It's all right—it'll be safe enough there.'

'Would you like me to go and get it for you?'

'No. It's all right.' She had spoken a little too sharply, and the girl looked taken aback. Drawing a steadying breath, she tried to force herself to relax. 'Thank you, Judy, but really, it'll be quite safe.'

'Can we have a voice-level, please, Rachel?' the floor manager called.

The make-up girl faded from the set, and Rachel cleared her throat, and recited her introduction.

'That's fine. One minute.'

She smiled into the camera to ease her facial muscles, acutely conscious that under the hot studio lights every fleeting expression in her eyes would be revealed in brutal close-up. To focus her mind, she began mentally rehearsing her script—she always wrote the links herself, and timed them carefully before ever coming near the studio, so she barely needed the Autocue.

'Stand by.' The floor manager held up his two hands, and began counting down with precise timing. The red light on top of the remote-control Vidicon came on, and almost miraculously she felt her mind empty of everything but what she was doing. She leaned forward slightly, as if talking to just one person instead of several million, and as the floor manager's finger swept towards her she began.

'Good evening, and welcome to *In Review* . . .'

The taping went well; only one small segment had to be re-recorded. As soon as the floor manager signalled the studio-release Rachel escaped as quickly as she could from the set, with a brief word of thanks to the crew, and hurried upstairs to the small dressing-room she shared with the few other female presenters on the Arts and Current Affairs staffs.

Fortunately it was empty. With a weary sigh she sat down before the brightly lit mirror, and began to carefully remove every trace of the heavy maquillage needed for the television cameras—she hated the feel of it clogging her skin.

Her left hand felt naked without her ring. But she was going to have to steel herself for all the gossip—the news would be all round the studios in no time, and probably by this evening the Press would be on to it. At thirty-one, and notoriously single, she knew that what she preferred to think of as the trashier end of the media seemed to think that they had every right to intrude into her private life, just because she regularly appeared on television. Unable to uncover any juicy secrets about her, they had portrayed her as aloof, even a little frosty. The news of her engagement had made the front pages of several tabloids—it had been a poor week for real news that week. Its ending was likely to stir similar interest, even more unwelcome.

She slicked on the light everyday make-up that she preferred, and changed quickly into a smartly tailored business suit, packing the burgundy silk outfit carefully into a garment bag and hanging it on the rail. Then, picking up her briefcase, she stepped out into the corridor.

Simon was waiting for her. She hesitated for a fatal moment, reluctant to face him, and he took swift advantage of her uncertainty, stepping forward, trapping her against the wall. 'Rache...'

She turned her face away, pain and anger warring inside her. 'Leave me alone, Simon,' she pleaded tautly. 'I've nothing more to say to you.'

'We can't just leave it like this, Rache,' he argued, a low note of urgency in his voice. 'We had a good relationship...'

'"Had",' she repeated pointedly. 'Past tense.'

'*Why?* Believe me, Linda wasn't important. It's you I love...'

'Then why did you go with her?' she demanded, turning on him an accusing glare.

He shrugged his wide shoulders, shaking his head. 'I don't know,' he admitted wryly. 'It was just... Maybe if you and I...'

'Oh, so it's my fault, is it?' she threw at him, her voice bitter.

'Well, it is rather a lot to ask of a man, in this day and age,' he protested, those dark eyes smiling down into hers.

She turned away from him again, determined not to let him weaken her resolve. 'Three more weeks,' she countered, the sharp tears stinging the backs of her eyes. 'Was that so long to wait?'

'We have been engaged since Christmas,' he pointed out.

'I thought you understood—I thought you agreed with me.'

He laughed with a trace of sardonic self-mockery. 'Well, yes... I mean, it was a lovely, romantic idea. But in real life... well, I suppose I just wasn't as strong as I thought I was.'

She hesitated, his words causing her an uncomfortable pang of self-doubt. Why *had* she insisted so firmly that they should wait until after they were married before they slept together? Surely, if she loved him, it should have been natural that she would want to be as close, as intimate with him as possible?

But she wasn't used to being close to people; that wall of reserve with which she had surrounded herself for so long had become in effect her prison—she didn't know how to break it down.

Cautiously she slanted a glance up at the man beside her. Maybe she hadn't been quite fair on him; it must have been hard at times—that Linda probably hadn't been the first to offer him the temptation to stray. He was very good-looking—tall and dark, with strong aquiline features that showed unmistakably the intelligence and drive that had taken him to an executive position with the television company, though he was only thirty-eight.

But she was just too hurt to forgive him. Shaking her head, she pushed past him. 'No, Simon, I'm sorry,' she insisted firmly. 'It's over. I wish you well, but I'm not going to change my mind. Goodnight.'

He reached out to catch her arm, but at that moment another door opened further down the corridor, and a number of people spilled out. Rachel felt a breath of relief—Simon was certainly not the sort to risk making a scene in public. She made her escape quickly, down in the lift and right out of the building.

In her agitated frame of mind, it was fortunate that it was only a short drive to her new apartment—the apartment she was to have shared with Simon after they were married. It was in one of the most prestigious riverside developments in London's Docklands, right in the heart of the city. The building was a converted wharf that had been completely gutted and rebuilt inside, while retaining the solid Victorian exterior.

It was so new that the contractor's men were still working on it—a gaggle of them were standing around wasting time in front of the security gate which guarded the private underground car park, and she had to blare her horn to get them to move out of the way.

Several of them slanted her leering glances as they stepped aside to let her pass. Usually she would have been able to ignore their provocation, but today she flashed them a fulminating glare, and banged her foot sharply on the accelerator, the squeal of her tyres echoing in the hollow vaults of the car park as she swung the sleek silver Scimitar down the ramp and into her reserved space.

Snatching up her briefcase, she slammed the car door, and marched briskly over to the lift. She had to get a grip on herself—but it had been so unexpected, so hurtful... *Simon*, of all people! She had trusted him... 'Damn, damn, damn him,' she muttered fiercely, jabbing the call-button with one scarlet-tipped finger. 'Damn every man in Christendom to hell and beyond.'

'Well, that's a pretty sweeping statement.'

She twisted round sharply, and found herself looking up into a pair of mocking blue-grey eyes that were regarding her with insolent approval. She favoured him with her frostiest glare, but he was apparently impervious. He just went on with that lazy survey, assessing every inch.

She'd seen him before. He must be one of the contractor's men—an electrician, to judge by the heavy coil of cable slung casually over his shoulder. And he obviously thought he was God's gift to women—not without some justification, she conceded dispassionately. If you liked that type.

He was tall—though she stood almost six feet in her high-heeled shoes, she had to look up at him. His blond hair curled rough and untamed, but his features were carved with the perfection of Adonis. He was wearing a motorbike jacket, adorned with casually stitched labels and showing distinct signs of wear, the soft red leather moulded by the powerful breadth of his shoulders—and his jeans too had seen better days.

Her critical regard seemed to afford him some amusement. Hard white teeth gleamed as he flashed her a provocative smile. 'What's up, princess?' he enquired. 'The boyfriend been messing you about? I'll tell you what—why don't you chuck him over, and take up with me instead? I reckon we could have a great time together.'

Well, she certainly had to give him ten out of ten for cheek! But the last thing she needed at the moment was some arrogant cockney electrician trying to chat her up. With chilly disdain she responded, 'No, thank you,' and turned him an aloof shoulder as the lift arrived.

She stepped into it, and he followed her, the doors sliding shut behind him. She could still feel his eyes resting on her, and she held herself very erect, trying her best to ignore him—though that was far from easy in the confined space of the lift. He had a way of looking at her that made her feel acutely conscious of every curve of her body, as if the tailored lines of her suit were somehow far too soft and clinging.

The lift reached her floor, and the doors slid open, but instead of standing aside to let her pass he leaned out one hand against the wall, barring her way. 'I'm not a bad proposition, you know,' he persisted, his eyes mocking her. 'I've got all my own teeth.'

'I really don't have the slightest interest in your attributes,' she returned, at her most haughty. 'Now if you'll kindly excuse me...?'

She brushed past him, bristling, all too aware as she stalked across the carpeted hall of the way the high, spiked heels of her shoes emphasised the graceful sway of her hips as she walked. She could almost feel the heat of his insolent gaze riveted to the motion of her neat derrière, moulded by her pencil-slim skirt.

Behind her she heard him laugh softly. 'Stuck-up bitch, aren't you?' he remarked cordially. 'Still, if you change your mind about taking up with me, just knock on the ceiling—I'll be right upstairs.'

She didn't deign to answer that parting shot, and the closing lift doors removed his irritating presence. She let herself into her apartment and closed the door.

The tension inside her really was giving her a headache. With a weary sigh she dropped her briefcase on an armchair, and strolled across the room to stand gazing out of the wide window at the spectacular view of the Thames.

The sun was shining on the wide river, turning it to a ribbon of shimmering steel. To her right rose the famous landmark of Tower Bridge, and across on the far bank the gleaming glass and concrete blocks of the city office towers soared majestically against the blue summer sky.

They had chosen this apartment together, she and Simon. It had been exactly what they had wanted—it was convenient for the studio, the block had superb facilities, including a swimming-pool and a fully equipped private health club in the basement, and there were some very good restaurants and shops in the cobbled courtyard downstairs.

Turning, she cast her eye around the room. It was a beautiful apartment. Not large—it had only one bedroom—but now that she would be continuing to live here by herself that would be an advantage. The stark simplicity of a gleaming beechwood floor and plain white walls perfectly complemented her stylish black-leather-upholstered Italian furniture. Her well-tended collection of pot plants added a welcome touch of greenery, and she had one good picture on the wall—a limited-edition etching by Lowry, rendered before he had found fame with his naïve industrial landscapes.

A sudden wave of loneliness washed over her, and she sank her head forward against the cool window-pane and closed her eyes. In just five weeks' time Simon would have been moving in here with her, when they returned from the romantic honeymoon in Venice they had planned.

He had seemed so right for her—why had it all had to go so wrong? She had known him for five years, since he had found her working for a local radio station in her native Manchester, and persuaded her to come to London to front his new arts programme. She had been nervous of television at first, but he had been her guide and mentor, shaping her style, refining her tastes; he had taught her all she knew.

It had been only gradually that their professional relationship had developed into something closer. But on Christmas Eve he had proposed—so romantically, in the moonlit garden of her parents' home. And at last she had begun to hope that she could find the security and happiness that she had so envied other women. Though he had been married before—he had been divorced for eight years—he still maintained a cordial relationship with his ex-wife, and regularly saw his daughter, now thirteen. Surely that was a point in his favour?

And now she was going to have to break the news to everyone. Her mother would be far from pleased—the wedding was all arranged, the guests invited, the cake ordered, the cars and the photographers booked. All that worry and expense... Not that it had been her idea to do it all on such a grand scale—after all, since Simon was divorced, it was only to be a civil ceremony. But her mother wouldn't be dissuaded—she had waited many years to play the role of 'mother of the bride'. And she had been absolutely charmed by Simon.

With a sigh Rachel picked up the telephone, but put it down again without dialling. She'd ring later, when she felt a little better. What she needed now was a nice strong cup of coffee. But all of fate was obviously conspiring against her today— the kettle wasn't working. Cursing to herself, she tried it in another socket, but still nothing happened. Just to check that it wasn't the kettle that was at fault, she tried plugging in the juicer, but that wasn't working either.

'Of all the... It's that damned electrician working upstairs,' she muttered furiously.

'Stupid, incompetent...' Whatever he was doing up there, he had somehow managed to interfere with the wiring in her kitchen. A surge of righteous indignation made her forget her usual reserve, and she slammed out of the flat, intent on going up to the penthouse and giving the arrogant young man a piece of her mind.

She had to bang three times on the door before she got any response. At last he opened it; he had taken off his leather jacket, and was wearing a black T-shirt, stretched taut across the hard muscles in his shoulders. Standing there leaning casually against the door-frame, so disconcertingly male... Her mouth felt suddenly dry, and she almost forgot what she had come for.

But, as she had anticipated, he greeted her with an insolently mocking smile. 'Well, hello there, princess. Changed your mind already?' he taunted, letting his eyes drift down over her body in a survey so intimate it brought a tinge of pink to her cheeks.

She stiffened in instinctive defence, returning him an icy glare. 'You've done something to the electricity in my kitchen,' she informed him coldly. 'Nothing's working.'

He laughed, raising his hands in a playful gesture of innocence. 'Not guilty,' he protested. 'Sure it's not just the fuse?'

'No, it isn't the fuse!'

'Did you look?'

She caught herself up, struggling to control the anger exploding inside her. 'No,' she conceded tersely.

'Then perhaps you'd better check that, before you start throwing accusations around,' he suggested, an inflexion of sardonic humour in his voice.

She hesitated. He was right, of course—she should have thought of that herself. Already she was beginning to regret the heated impulse that had brought her storming up here—anger was an emotion that she didn't trust. 'Of...of course.' She drew back a step, fixing one of her cool smiles in place, ready to retreat. 'I didn't think of that. I'm sorry to have bothered you...'

'You know how to deal with a fuse-box?' he asked.

'Well...er...'

'Hold on a tick while I get a screwdriver.'

'Oh, I couldn't possibly impose...' she protested quickly.

He smiled. 'It won't take me a minute,' he pointed out. 'If you get someone out of *Yellow Pages*, you might have to wait in for a couple of days before they show up.'

Reluctantly she had to concede that he was right again—she knew from experience how inconvenient it could be. 'Well...thank you,' she accepted with a stiff nod. 'It's very kind of you.'

'No trouble.' He smiled with just a hint of mockery, and turned back into the apartment.

She waited on the threshold, peering curiously into what she could see of the room. She knew from the architect's drawings that the penthouse was enormous, covering most of the top floor of this block. The design was open-plan, on two levels, beneath the roof-space. The walls were of natural brick, and the original heavy oak beams had been left as a sculptural feature. All along one side of the room were bronzed glass panels that could be slid open to give access to a wide roof-terrace overlooking the river.

It was very much a man's apartment. Rachel was intrigued. Whoever had bought it must have paid a fortune for it. But somehow it didn't have the air of a place that was to be used only for business purposes—for meetings, or to entertain clients. It bore the stamp of a strong personality, too distinctive to be the work of an interior design consultant.

The electrician strolled back in from the roof-terrace, sliding the glass door shut behind him. 'The name's Nick, by the way,' he introduced himself, slanting her a friendly smile.

He really did have rather a nice smile, she had to concede. It lit up his blue-grey eyes with a wicked glint, and she couldn't help but smile in response. After all, since he had been so kind as to offer to help her, the least she could do was be pleasant to him. And his casual flirtation was really quite harmless—it was probably just his way of trying to be friendly.

'I'm Rachel,' she responded, letting herself unfreeze a little.

'I know—Rachel Haston. I've seen you on the box. What's the name of it—*In Review*?'

'That's right.'

'Not really my cup of tea,' he admitted cheerfully. 'I only watch it to see you.'

She laughed, accustomed to such remarks. 'I'm very flattered.'

'You look even better in the flesh,' he added, letting his eyes drift down over her in another leisurely appraisal. 'A real classy bird.'

She should have been annoyed, but somehow his humour robbed his words of offence. 'Thank you,' she conceded, a hint of ironic amusement in her voice.

The lift arrived at her floor, and she let him into her apartment. He glanced around with casual interest. 'Nice gaff,' he approved. 'You live here on your own?'

'Y...yes.'

He didn't seem to notice her hesitation as he strolled over to take a look out of the window. 'You can hardly believe the changes around here,' he mused, his head tilted to one side as he surveyed the rows of newly renovated wharfs along the riverside. 'It used to be all derelict—just a load of old warehouses.'

Rachel was watching him warily. Maybe she shouldn't have let him into the apartment—and she certainly shouldn't have told him that she lived alone. After all, she didn't know for sure that he worked for the contractor. He could be a burglar...or worse...

He turned away from the window. 'So—let's take a look at this fuse-box,' he suggested, flashing her a friendly smile.

'Oh...' She pulled herself together quickly. 'Yes, it's here, by the door.'

It took him only a few minutes to diagnose what was wrong. 'It's the circuit-breaker,' he told her.

'Can you fix it?'

'Of course—it's just a matter of turning it back on again. But that's not the problem. You must have an overload somewhere in your kitchen. A short circuit,' he explained as she looked faintly puzzled. 'I'll have to find that and fix it for you, or it'll just go again.'

'Will it take long?'

'That depends on where it is.'

She followed him into the kitchen, adopting an air of detached interest as she watched him check the plug on her kettle. But she was aware of a strange disturbance in the even pattern of her heartbeat. It wasn't that she was afraid of him, in spite of her doubts—somehow he didn't seem the sort who would try to force himself on her. The threat he posed was not so direct...

'Nothing wrong there...' He started checking the sockets, and almost at once he let out a satisfied, 'Ah!'

'Have you found it?' she enquired anxiously.

'Uh-huh. Look at that—the wires are touching. It's causing a short—no wonder it burnt out the circuit-breaker.'

She leaned over to peer at the wires he was pointing out with the tip of his screwdriver. She could see exactly what he meant—the screws inside the socket weren't fastened properly, allowing the wires to work loose, and the insulating plastic around one of the wires had started to char.

But her mind wasn't on plugs and sockets. Standing so close to him, her arm almost brushing his, she was almost overpoweringly aware of the sheer impact of all that raw masculinity. She drew away from him quickly, her mouth dry. 'Well! What shoddy workmanship,' she protested a little too emphatically. 'I ought to complain to the contractors about that.'

'So you should,' he agreed readily, with all the contempt of a craftsman for a badly done job. 'That's just slipshod.'

It didn't take him long to repair the socket— he worked deftly, and as she watched him she noticed that his hands weren't rough and grimy, as she had imagined, but well-kept, with long, slim fingers and strong wrists. He screwed the socket cover back into place, and went to turn on the electricity.

'There you are,' he announced with a flourish as the orange light on the kettle glowed.

'Thank you. Er...would you like a cup of coffee?' she invited politely.

'That would be very nice.'

He was leaning against the breakfast bar, watching her again, a hint of speculation in his smile. She turned away from him quickly, an odd glow of warmth in her cheeks. What on earth had made her offer him coffee? She had had no intention of giving him any excuse to linger—she didn't want him to get any ideas.

She got out another cup. 'Milk and sugar?' she enquired, trying to instil a note of cool formality into her voice.

'Yes, please.'

Her hand was shaking slightly as she spooned out the coffee. If only he wouldn't look at her like that... Suddenly all sorts of disturbing images were swirling in her brain, and she couldn't push them away. He laughed softly, as if he was fully aware of what was in her mind, and, coming up close behind her, he took the spoon from her numb fingers and put it down on the breakfast bar.

She stiffened as she felt the brush of his finger-tips on her arms. When had she ever given him permission to touch her? But as he turned her slowly round to face him, she found herself gazing up into those ever-changing sea-grey eyes, and she felt as if she were drowning. He was going to kiss her—and he knew that she wasn't going to even try to stop him.

'A real classy bird,' he murmured huskily.

His head bent slowly over hers, and the first brush of his lips sent a sizzling heat right through

her. She closed her eyes, her blood swirling dizzily
in her brain. He met not a shred of resistance as
his tongue swirled deep into her mouth, plundering every sweet, secret corner with a flagrant
sensuality that left her helpless.

He was moving against her, curving her back
against the breakfast bar so that every inch of
her body was offered intimately to his, and she
had lifted her arms around his neck, surrendering wantonly to his kiss. There was no way
she could control the quivering response inside
her, and it communicated itself plainly to him;
he lifted his head, a glint of triumph in his eyes.

She stared up at him, her breathing ragged,
stunned by the impact of what was happening to
her. She had never known anything like this
before. Even with Simon...

Simon! A shock of guilt stabbed at her heart,
and she drew back, horrified. What was she
*doing*? And with a man she had never met
before... He recognised her sudden resistance at
once, and let her go. She turned quickly away
from him, her cheeks flaming scarlet.

The kettle had boiled, and with a supreme
effort of will she pulled herself together, turning
all her attention to making the coffee. Maybe if
she tried to behave as if nothing had happened... She stole a covert glance at him from
beneath her lashes. He was leaning casually
against the worktop, watching her watching him,
a faintly quizzical smile on his handsome face.
She looked away again quickly.

Of course, it was all Simon's fault. She had had no conscious intention of paying him back at his own game, but some irrational part of her mind must have been planning something like this. It was a stupid thing to have done, but the worst thing she could do now would be to panic. She had to try to remain cool at all costs, and just get rid of him as quickly as she could.

Drawing a deep, steadying breath, she forced a rather brittle smile into place and turned to hand him his coffee. 'There you are,' she said brightly. 'By the way, how much do I owe you?'

He lifted one questioning eyebrow. 'Well, that's the first time anyone's ever offered to pay me,' he taunted, deliberately provocative.

She returned him an icy glare. 'I meant for fixing the wiring,' she enunciated in a glacial tone.

He laughed, shaking his head. 'You don't have to pay me for that, princess—just call it a neighbourly gesture.'

'But...' *Neighbourly?* What did he mean by...?

'Who did you think I was?' he asked, his voice ripe with amusement. 'The electrician?'

'Well... aren't you?'

'No. I'm moving in upstairs.'

'Into the *penthouse*?'

He nodded. 'One of my companies owns the block.'

## CHAPTER TWO

RACHEL stared at him, momentarily stunned. Of course...*that* was why he had seemed familiar—she must have seen his face in the newspapers and on television countless times. His name was...Farlowe—Nick Farlowe. She shook her head, laughing at her own stupidity. The man was certainly no electrician—he was a very clever financial manipulator, and reputed to be worth millions.

'I'm sorry,' she breathed, bemused. 'I just didn't recognise you. You must think I'm a real idiot.'

He laughed, a speculative glint in those wicked eyes. 'Only if you still won't go out with me,' he teased.

She felt a blush of pink rise to her cheeks. It was one thing to indulge in a little...harmless dalliance with some cheeky workman whom she would more than likely never see again, but this situation could be potentially fraught with complications. She studied him covertly from beneath her lashes as he lounged against the breakfast bar, drinking his coffee.

The story went that he'd started out in the scrap-metal business while he was supposed to be still at school, and he'd made his first million by the time he was twenty. He was still only twenty-nine, but already he'd multiplied that figure many times over, mainly by speculating on the futures market.

He had the golden touch, they said—he couldn't go wrong. Of course, that had become a self-fulfilling prophecy now—whatever he bought, the punters would follow, automatically pushing up the prices of the shares. He must be laughing all the way to the bank.

He had the golden touch with women too, they said. He just had to snap his fingers... She could well believe it—she'd almost fallen for it herself! He was still watching her, his eyes alight with a look of amused enquiry as he waited for her response to his casual invitation. She chose to evade the issue entirely.

'So why were you doing your own wiring?' she challenged, trying to inject a light note into her voice. 'Are you one of those penny-pinching millionaires who won't spend a farthing if they don't have to?'

He laughed, shaking his head. 'Not at all. I'm just rigging some lighting for the roof-garden, and it was as easy to do it myself as to explain to somebody else what I wanted.'

'Ah, I see——' A loud rap on the door interrupted her. Rachel frowned, puzzled—there was a video-intercom from the main entrance, and no one could get into the building without passing scrutiny from the security personnel downstairs. 'Who on earth...?'

'Shall I answer it for you?' Nick offered at once.

'No—it's all right...' An uncomfortable suspicion was already forming in her mind. She put down her cup, and went over to open the door.

Simon was standing in the hall, a large bouquet of red roses in his hands. He met her frozen expression with a slightly crooked smile. 'Hello, Rache,' he said, holding out the flowers.

'What are you doing here?' she demanded, flustered. 'How did you get past the security?'

'I told him my tale, and he felt sorry for me,' he explained, laughing in wry self-mockery. 'I had to come, Rache.' There was a low note of urgency in his voice. 'We couldn't talk this afternoon——'

'We've nothing to talk about,' she insisted stiffly. 'Go away, Simon. I don't want to see you.'

'Rache...' He stepped forward, pressing the roses into her arms and bearing her back into the flat. 'You can't go on——'

'Got a problem here, princess?' Nick was lounging one wide shoulder against the frame of the kitchen door, his coffee-cup still in his hand, apparently very much at home. But, though he appeared totally relaxed, there was a hint of steely warning underlying his tone.

Simon looked startled. 'Who the hell are you?' he demanded, glaring at him belligerently.

'I'm a friend of Rachel's,' Nick responded in that same deceptively mild drawl. 'I didn't hear her invite you in.'

Simon put his arm around her waist, drawing her close against him in a possessive gesture. 'I don't have to wait on an invitation,' he countered, his jaw set in a hard line. 'Rachel and I are...were...'

'Oh, yes?' Nick flickered a glance at her pale face. 'Looks like one of us ought to be leaving, princess. Do you want me to go, or shall I get rid of him for you?'

'No—I can deal with it,' she insisted, breaking free of Simon's grasp. 'Simon, please,' she begged. 'I told you this afternoon—it's over between us. Just leave me alone.'

'It isn't over, and you know it,' he insisted forcefully. 'I know I hurt you—it was unforgivable of me——'

'Simon, *please*...'

He put his hands on her shoulders, compelling her to look up into his face. 'Just give me another chance, Rache——'

Nick's voice cut ruthlessly across the scene. 'The lady told you to go,' he reminded him tersely. 'Would you like some assistance?'

Simon's eyes flared with anger, and for a tense moment the two men faced each other, spoiling for a fight. They were well matched for size and weight, and the outcome would have been hard to predict. But fortunately Simon wasn't the sort to embarrass Rachel by indulging in an unseemly brawl.

'Very well, I'm going,' he conceded with dignity. He glanced down at her, those dark eyes conveying an unspoken message. 'Goodbye, Rache,' he murmured. 'I'll see you tomorrow.'

With a last hostile glare in Nick's direction he stalked out, closing the door behind him with a controlled slam. Rachel stood staring at it for a moment, her mind numb. Of all the awkward things to happen . . .

'Well,' remarked Nick, an inflexion of sardonic humour in his voice. 'Who was that?'

With the speed of deep-ingrained instinct she retreated behind her rock-wall of defence. 'Oh . . . just a friend,' she responded with dignity.

He lifted one sardonic eyebrow. 'A friend?' He flickered a quizzical glance over the roses in her hands.

'We . . . were engaged,' she conceded stiffly.

'I see.'

She walked past him into the kitchen, and began to search through the cupboards for a vase to put the roses in. 'We were due to get married in three weeks' time,' she informed him, her voice carefully flattened of all emotion. 'But I found out that he was seeing someone else.'

'So you ditched him?'

'Yes.'

He laughed drily. 'Well, I'm sorry if I stood in the way of a lovers' reconciliation,' he said. 'You should have told me.'

She shook her head in quick denial. 'Oh, no. It was . . . nothing like that.'

'But he said he'll see you tomorrow?'

'He works at the studio,' she explained briefly. 'He's an executive producer.'

'Ah. So he could make things fairly awkward for you if he wanted to.'

He spoke with an unexpectedly gentle concern, and her nerves were so taut-strung that for one dangerous moment she felt an urge to reach for the comfort he seemed to offer. She suppressed it ruthlessly, the strain telling in her voice.

'Not at all—he's no longer directly involved with my programme. And besides,' she added, all the more frostily because she had been secretly fearing herself that the next few weeks were going to be extremely difficult, 'Simon wouldn't dream of doing anything like that—he's far too much of a gentleman.'

He flashed one of those wicked smiles, an unrepentant sinner. 'Oh, well, now that's something I've never pretended to be,' he taunted. 'What you see is what you get.'

There was an explicit invitation—a challenge—in his eyes, but Rachel refused to meet it. She looked away, struggling to maintain her façade of dignified composure.

He laughed softly, with just a hint of lazy mockery. 'Well, I'd better be going,' he conceded, draining his coffee and putting down his cup. 'You shouldn't have any more trouble with that wiring now.'

'If I do, I'll get in touch with the agents,' she responded coolly as she followed him to the door to see him out. 'Thank you for your help.'

'No trouble.'

On the threshold he paused deliberately, so that she found herself suddenly far too close to him. His eyes focused speculatively on her lips, and she felt her heartbeat accelerate alarmingly. Some powerful, primeval force that she didn't understand seemed to be holding her captive, binding her will. She fought to resist, the hectic flush of her cheeks betraying the heat in her blood.

He smiled slowly, as if he knew all too well that he was creating havoc inside her. But he made no move to touch her. He simply drawled a lazy, 'See you around then, princess,' and, scorning the lift, he took the stairs to the upper floor two at a time.

She closed the door, struggling to steady her ragged breathing. What on earth had got into her, to behave like that? He wasn't even her type, for goodness' sake! She preferred a certain sophistication, a certain refinement—that sort of blatant animal magnetism had never much appealed to her.

She laughed wryly, shaking her head. All those angry accusations she had hurled at Simon, and now she had behaved just as badly herself! Could she really condemn him for his moment of weakness? Except that in his case it hadn't exactly been a moment, she reminded herself bitterly. By all accounts, it had been going on for several weeks. All those nights he had claimed to be so busy!

What had been the attraction of that Linda anyway? She was nothing special to look at—if anything, she was quite dumpy, and her hair could certainly benefit from the attention of a decent stylist... But, of course, it wasn't her looks that had been important, she reminded herself with a bitter smile. Linda was the sort of girl the magazines talked about in those articles— 'Have You Got IT?'

And whatever 'IT' was, she reflected with dry amusement, she was fairly sure that she herself had been at the back of the queue when they were handing it out. She had never really understood what all the fuss was about. When she was younger there had been a few boys, but their clumsy eagerness had very much put her off. And then with Simon—well, it hadn't really been that sort of relationship...

With a sudden vivid clarity that almost took her breath away, she felt again the sizzling heat of Nick Farlowe's kiss. She touched her finger-tips to her lips, feeling their unusual warmth. She had never dreamed that a kiss could be like that, or that she could respond with such over-whelming passion...

Startled and frightened by the implications of that thought, she pushed it firmly from her mind. She had been upset at the time, that was all, and more vulnerable than usual. It had been no more than an illusion—maybe he had been eating chilli-peppers! Laughing at her own nonsense, she went into the kitchen to make herself another cup of coffee.

'So, we'll go with the statement from the Arts Council, and hold the piece on the National Theatre until next week. OK, Rachel?'

'What? Oh . . . yes, fine.' She smiled brightly, not at all sure what she had just agreed to. It wasn't like her to allow her mind to wander during a production meeting, but her emotions hadn't been in such a mess for a very long time.

Of course, the news of her broken engagement was all round the studios already. Oh, no one had been crass enough to actually mention the subject—it was in the careful way they had all said, 'Good morning', the way they watched her as if she were a time-bomb that might explode at any moment.

And most people would know the cause of the split as well. The only surprise was that it had taken her so long to find out—the studio gossip-machine usually worked much more efficiently than that!

*Had* she been a little hasty with Simon? She had lain awake most of the night, tossing things around in her mind. Her own lapse had made her view his indiscretion in a slightly less critical light. And he seemed to be genuinely sorry, he said he still loved her—but could she ever trust him again?

The production meeting was coming to an end; people were checking their diaries and coordinating schedules. Someone engaged Rachel's attention with a question, and the telephone rang. She hesitated, trying to deal with everything at once, uncharacteristically disorganised.

It was Simon's voice on the other end of the line, and she temporised with a quick, 'Would you hang on for a moment?' and turned back to Gerald. 'Yes, I'm hoping to get the Arts Minister to agree to an interview next week. His secretary's ringing me back later this morning.'

Gerald nodded. 'Good. Keep at it—we don't want to let him off the hook now.'

'I'll do my best,' she promised. That brief respite had given her a chance to regather some of her composure. She swung her chair round so that she was half turned away from the other people in the room, and spoke quietly into the receiver. 'Yes, Simon?'

She heard his wry laughter. 'Well, at least you didn't just slam the phone down on me.'

'I'm sorry. We were just finishing a meeting,' she explained, keeping her voice carefully neutral, both to convey to him that she was still of the same mind and so that if anyone behind her was trying to eavesdrop they would learn little of interest.

'Will you have dinner with me tonight?' he asked.

'No, Simon,' she responded, though her words lacked some of the certainty she had felt yesterday. 'There's no point—there's nothing more for us to talk about.'

'Isn't there?' An edge of sarcasm had crept into his voice. 'I don't agree with you. Maybe I'd like to know what Nicholas Farlowe was doing in *our* apartment yesterday afternoon? Oh, yes, I know who he was,' he added drily. 'I recognised him at once.'

Guilt generated a surge of answering anger inside her. 'I really don't think it's any of your business,' she snapped back.

'Oh, isn't it? I know his reputation—who doesn't? You accuse me of being unfaithful, and all the time you've been seeing him behind my back.'

'I have not been seeing him!' Suddenly she realised that she had been raising her voice. She slanted an anxious glance back over her shoulder, but most people were already drifting out of the production office. 'I haven't been seeing him,' she repeated in a more restrained tone. 'For your information, he's just moved into the penthouse. I only met him yesterday—I happened to be having a spot of trouble with the electricity, and he was kind enough to fix it for me.'

'I see.' There was still a terseness in his voice. 'Very well—I'm sorry. I was so jealous, seeing you with him, I suppose I just jumped to conclusions. I guess it would have served me right, after the way I treated you,' he added wryly.

She bit her lip, remembering all too vividly what had happened with Nick. 'Apology accepted,' she murmured, uncomfortable with the knowledge that she was the one deceiving him this time.

'Listen, Rache, at least give us a chance to talk it over,' he pleaded. 'Let me take you out to dinner. No strings, I promise. Just to talk. Then if you still say it's over, I'll accept it.'

She hesitated, struggling with the turmoil of emotions inside her. She didn't want to give him the opportunity to persuade her, against her better judgement, and yet... she didn't want it to end on such acrimonious terms. Perhaps they could at least remain friends...?

'I... I can't make it until Saturday,' she temporised. 'I've a deadline tomorrow for eight hundred words, and I'll be working on it all evening. And then tomorrow I'm going down to Glyndebourne to record an interview with Maria Ewing. I won't be back till quite late on Friday.'

'Saturday will be fine,' he agreed readily. 'I'll pick you up at eight o'clock.'

'OK, Simon. I'll see you then.'

'Goodbye, darling. And just remember one thing—I love you, always.'

Rachel couldn't answer. She held the receiver for a minute, and then put it down carefully on its rest. Already she was beginning to regret that she had agreed to go out with him—it would only encourage him to think that she would yield to further pressure.

She *did* have an article to write—one of several that she regularly contributed to a number of magazines and newspapers. But it was virtually finished—it wouldn't take her much more than an hour or so of work. But she knew that if she had told Simon that she was actually playing squash with her sister-in-law, Maggie, he would have tried to persuade her to break the arrangement.

But she enjoyed her Wednesday afternoons with Maggie. They usually got together for a game of squash, or sometimes if they were feeling lazy they would go shopping instead. Maggie was one of the few women she had ever been able to be friends with—perhaps because there was no shadow of jealousy or competition between them.

They had hit it off from the moment her brother had introduced them, some ten years ago now. It wouldn't have been easy for any bride that Richard had chosen to handle a potentially very domineering mother-in-law, but Maggie had managed it with a twist of humour that had won her a fond place in everyone's heart.

As soon as Rachel opened the door of her flat, she knew she had no need to tell Maggie what had happened. 'I had the Dragon on the phone for over an hour last night,' she announced wryly, throwing her arms around her in an impulsive hug.

Rachel laughed in sympathy. 'Oh, Maggie, I'm sorry. Did you get the full brunt of it?' she asked.

'The whole shebang. But how are you? You look all right.' Maggie held Rachel at arm's length and surveyed her with a critical eye. 'My goodness, I'd kill for your figure,' she sighed. 'I only have to *look* at a plate of chips! So what happened? Your mother's version was somewhat garbled.'

'Oh, we just ... decided to call the whole thing off,' Rachel explained lightly.

Maggie's eyes sharpened. 'Hey, come on—this is me, remember? The truth, the whole truth and nothing but the truth, please.'

Rachel sighed. 'He was seeing someone else,' she confessed. 'I just found out yesterday.'

'What? Oh, the *rat*! Well, it's a good job you found out *before* the wedding.'

'I suppose so,' Rachel conceded wistfully.

Maggie stared at her. 'You don't mean you could actually *forgive* him for it, do you?' she demanded, indignant.

'Well ... No, not really, but ... Oh, I don't know. It's not very nice to be back on the shelf again.'

'Back on the shelf? What ever gave you that idea?' protested Maggie bracingly. 'With the way you look, you should be knocking 'em dead in the aisles.'

'Looks aren't everything,' Rachel pointed out with a crooked little smile.

'No—but you've got a darned sight more to offer besides. You're bright, and sweet-natured, and generous. Don't worry—there are plenty more fish in the sea.'

Rachel shook her head, laughing. 'Oh, I don't think so—not for me. I think I'll just concentrate on my career from now on. Besides, who wants to marry a fish?'

They were both laughing as they rode down in the lift to the health-club complex in the basement of the block. There were two squash courts, situated next to the hydro-gym and opposite the swimming-pool. The facilities were all designed with the same eye for style as the rest of the building, linked by a pleasant lounge area, with comfortable seating. The brick walls and pinewood ceiling, and the clusters of thriving green plants beneath sculptural spotlighting, created a pergola effect that was very restful.

Both courts were in use, and Rachel's heart gave an odd little thud as she realised that one of the players was Nick Farlowe. He was wearing white shorts and T-shirt, and his muscles were hard and defined beneath gleaming sun-bronzed skin. He was moving around the court with the grace of a natural athlete, and she found herself watching him as if mesmerised.

She looked away again quickly, hoping Maggie hadn't noticed her reaction. *Careful, Rachel,* she warned herself sharply. It wasn't like her to let herself be affected in this way by the sight of a male body, even if she had rarely seen one in quite such superb condition.

Maggie was making no effort to disguise her admiration. 'Mmm hmm!' she murmured approvingly. 'Who's that?'

'Oh . . . His name's Nick Farlowe—you know, the scrap-metal king.' Rachel was trying to speak lightly, but her own ear caught the slight tremor in her voice. 'He's just moved in upstairs—apparently he's behind the property company that owns this block.'

'Really?' mused Maggie, watching him with unashamed interest. 'He must be rolling in it. Tasty, too. Is he married?'

'No,' conceded Rachel carefully. 'At least, not that I know of.'

'Hmm.' The scheming glint in her sister-in-law's eyes warned Rachel that she believed she had already located another 'fish'. Rachel shot her a warning glance—not with much hope of being attended to.

Maggie sat down on one of the upholstered benches to watch the two men play, and reluctantly Rachel sat down beside her. If she could have thought of some reasonable excuse, she would have suggested that they should forget about playing squash this afternoon after all, but Maggie would not easily be fooled. She leaned back, feigning casual relaxation, trying to pretend even to herself that she was interested only in the finer points of the match.

They were playing a hard game, with no mean skill. Nick's opponent was one of the other residents—something in banking. He had service, and hit a powerful backhand, keeping the trajectory high, and Nick volleyed it straight, a difficult ball close to the side-wall.

The ball flashed around the court, barely visible, rebounding fast off the walls, and the two men were competing fiercely for every single point. But Nick just had the upper hand. His technique was very good—he had an almost perfect position on the forehand, his feet still, his body inclined forward so that his head was well over the ball—and he had a mastery of tactics that would have been creditable for a professional.

He floated in a delicate drop-shot, played at an angle towards the nick, taking the pace out of the ball and catching his opponent out of position. The banker managed to return a rather desperate lob, but it lacked height, and Nick punished it with another very awkward cross-court drop, winning the point and the match.

Maggie applauded as the two men opened the perspex door and stepped out of the court. 'Very good,' she approved, with that easy friendliness that Rachel envied so much. 'I really enjoyed watching that.'

The banker was laughing. 'Rather more than I enjoyed playing it, I should imagine,' he admitted wryly. 'You're too good for me I'm afraid, Farlowe.'

Nick laughed, tossing his towel across his shoulder as he sat down casually opposite Rachel. 'Rubbish—you gave me a good game,' he countered. 'How are you fixed for Friday?'

The other man laughed again, mopping his face—he was flushed and breathless, while Nick had only the faintest gleam of sweat on his brow to show for his exertions. 'All right, then,' he agreed, raising his eyes heavenward. 'I must be a sucker for punishment. I reckon you'll have to accept a handicap, though—only shots above the line.'

Nick grinned. 'If you like,' he conceded easily. Those blue-grey eyes turned to Rachel, catching her off guard. 'Maybe we could get a mixed doubles going some time?' he suggested teasingly.

Somehow she managed to return him a cool smile, shaking her head. 'Oh, I don't think so,' she demurred, the faintest sliver of frost in her voice. 'Your standard of play would be far too good for us——'

'Don't be silly,' cut in Maggie promptly. 'We'll give you a game any time.'

Nick flashed her an appreciative smile, and turned back to Rachel, that wicked glint in his eyes. 'There you are,' he taunted, deliberately provocative.

Rachel shrugged, her expression schooled to convey the most supreme indifference. 'OK— we'll have to fix a date some time,' she conceded minimally.

'And if you wear that outfit,' he added, letting his gaze drift down over the length of her slender legs in a way that gave her the uncomfortable feeling that her brief tennis dress was far too short for decency, 'you'll have an unfair advantage. My mind won't be on the game at all.'

She flashed him a fulminating glare, but he was too thick-skinned to be deterred—he simply continued to survey her legs with undisguised appreciation, as if he had paid for the privilege. She felt a blush of pink rise to her cheeks, but she wasn't going to let him see that he had any effect on her.

'By the way, may I introduce my sister-in-law?' she remarked, seeking a way to divert his attention away from herself. 'Maggie—Nick Farlowe.'

The mocking glint in his eyes told her that he was wise to her ploy, but he turned to Maggie, warming her with the megawatt power of one of those devastating smiles. 'Hello—nice to meet you, Maggie. Do you work in television too?' he enquired with friendly interest.

Maggie's wedding-ring certainly conferred no immunity to the effects of that irresistible charm—she positively glowed in response. 'No—nothing so glamorous,' she sighed. 'I'm just a housewife.'

He laughed. 'I'm told that's a pretty full-time job.'

'It is—especially with a delinquent four-year-old, a manic dog, and a husband who doesn't know where the laundry-basket is!'

'Sounds like a lively household.'

Maggie gurgled, her eyes dancing flirtatiously. 'I'm thinking of joining the local rugby club as prop-forward, just so I can get a little peace and quiet on a Saturday afternoon!'

Rachel's lips thinned in annoyance as she watched them laughing together. Did Maggie *have* to make up to him like that? His ego was already quite inflated enough, without any extra encouragement. They seemed to have struck up a friendship with remarkable speed—already he was telling her that he was planning a house-warming party, and inviting her along.

'And your husband too, of course,' he added with a teasing reluctance.

'Oh, I'd love to come,' she sighed wistfully. 'But we're going up to visit my parents this weekend—it's their wedding anniversary.'

'Well, never mind. Another time, maybe?' He turned back to Rachel, so suddenly that he again caught her off guard. 'What about you, princess?' he enquired. 'Are you doing anything on Saturday night?'

She caught a sharp breath. 'Oh…I…I'm going out to dinner,' she stammered.

He smiled, arrogant enough to be untroubled by any competition. 'Well, bring him along too, then,' he suggested, a hint of challenge in his eyes. 'The more the merrier.'

She tilted her chin at a haughty angle. 'I hardly think so,' she countered stiffly.

He raised one eyebrow in sardonic enquiry. 'It's not that creep I met in your place yesterday, is it?' he taunted. She refused to meet his eyes, and he laughed mockingly. 'Well, I never—so the red roses did the trick after all, then? Maybe I should try it some time.'

She glared at him. 'Not that it's any of your business, but we're simply having dinner—as…friends,' she informed him with glacial emphasis.

He let his lip curl into something close to a sneer. 'Then bring him to my party,' he repeated, an edge of sarcasm in his voice.

'I'll see.' She turned him an aloof shoulder. 'We'd better start our game now the court's free,' she said to Maggie, 'or someone else will be sneaking in ahead of us.'

'Oh...yes, all right,' conceded Maggie, reluctant to let the exchange end—she had been attending with unabashed interest from the beginning. 'Goodbye, Nick. Nice to have met you,' she added, slanting him a wistful smile, and followed Rachel into the court. *'Well!'* she breathed as she closed the door. 'That is what I call very tasty indeed.'

Rachel managed a laugh. 'Maggie, you're a respectable married woman,' she reproved her mildly. 'You're not supposed to go around calling other men tasty.'

Maggie chuckled. 'Being married doesn't stop you *looking*. Besides, he seemed much more interested in you,' she added, her shrewd eyes watchful for any reaction.

Rachel shrugged her shoulders. 'Oh, I'm afraid he's interested in almost anything in a skirt,' she dismissed drily.

'Oh, come on!' protested Maggie, her eyes dancing. 'If I were single...'

Rachel shook her head. 'Anyway, he isn't really my type,' she insisted, tossing the ball up to serve. It was a weak shot, straight on to Maggie's volley, and she hit it dead.

She was still aware of Nick watching her from the shadows on the other side of the perspex screen, and it was difficult to put him out of her mind, particularly as she was so acutely concious that her tennis dress was short enough to offer him a glimpse of her neat derrière, alluringly packaged in trim white sports briefs, every time she bent over.

As she took up her position to serve again, she stole a quick glance in his direction. He was indeed watching her, lounging back in his seat and chatting casually to his friend, the faint smile on his handsome face telling her that he was thoroughly enjoying the view.

She felt a surge of fury rise inside her. She had always hated men who treated women simply as sex objects. Just because he was rich, and good-looking, he thought he could have any woman he wanted. Well, if he was planning to add her to his long list of conquests, he was in for a disappointment!

She slammed the ball viciously against the back wall, and it flew back straight on Maggie's body-line. She darted out of the way just in time, losing the point.

'Hey! Careful!' she protested, laughing.

'Sorry,' Rachel smiled wryly, pulling herself together with an effort of will. Nick Farlowe just wasn't worth wasting an ounce of anger on.

'So who are you going out with on Saturday?' Maggie asked as she retrieved the dead ball again.

'Simon.'

'What?' Maggie slanted her a look of surprise. 'I thought you said you'd finished with him?'

'I have. It's just . . . well, I don't want to part on bad terms with him. It's just the once—we agreed on that. I won't be going out with him again.'

Maggie's expression spoke volumes. 'If you ask me, you're nuts,' she declared firmly. 'If you haven't learned your lesson by now! And you pass up a hunk like that?' She nodded her head in Nick's direction.

'Nick Farlowe would hardly be a good bet for a stable relationship, with his track record,' Rachel pointed out drily.

'And you think Simon's a better bet?' challenged her sister-in-law with a touch of scorn. 'If you ask me, you had a lucky escape—a man who can't keep from checking if the grass is greener on the other side of the hill is *not* good husband material!'

'It wasn't like that,' protested Rachel, flushing. 'At least——'

'Three weeks before you were due to get married,' Maggie reminded her darkly. 'What do you think he'd be like after?'

'Yes, well . . . that would be different,' Rachel mumbled.

'Don't you believe it. If you can't trust him now, you can never trust him.'

# CHAPTER THREE

SATURDAY seemed to come round with alarming speed. Rachel spent all afternoon trying to decide what she would wear—she wanted to look her very best, just to make Simon realise what he had let slip through his fingers.

She changed three times before she was satisfied, finally settling on a pair of loose flowing trousers of black silk, and a clinging wrap-around top in shimmering shades of copper and bronze. She put her hair up in a sleekly elegant style, swirling it into a soft wave over her high forehead. Her only jewellery would be her heavy gold earrings—Simon had bought them for her at Christmas, but, after all, why shouldn't she wear them? He could read it any way he liked.

She was ready far too early, and pacing the floor, trying to sort out the confusion in her mind. She hadn't seen Simon since Wednesday, having been away from the studio, but the respite hadn't helped her decide whether she had been right to break off the engagement.

Part of her wanted desperately to set aside what had happened; before she had met Simon she had grown so accustomed to her spinster status that she had even believed herself to be content with it, but she was finding it much harder to readjust to it than she had anticipated.

After all, she argued with herself, had it been so very bad, what he had done? She had learned herself how easy it was to succumb to the fleeting temptation of physical attraction. They had had far more to their relationship than that; there was liking, and mutual respect—the kind of ingredients that really *mattered*. Surely they could build a successful marriage on that?

But Maggie's warning still whispered in her head. Myabe she had been right. Could Rachel really be sure that, once the honeymoon glow had worn off, there wouldn't be another Linda? And if she couldn't trust him, was there any future for them together?

And then there was Nick Farlowe. She hadn't spoken to him since Wednesday either, but she had seen him, down in the car park beneath the building. He'd been on his motorbike, a big powerful brute of a machine. She'd sat in her car, watching him ride in and park, watching him stroll over to the lift. He had a lithe, athletic way of moving, all male. She couldn't deny the strange fascination she felt, but she didn't like it. It made her feel uncomfortable——

The buzz of the video-intercom cut across her thoughts. The tiny screen showed her Simon's hazy black-and-white image, and she smiled to herself—he always looked good in formal evening clothes, and his black dinner-jacket and bow-tie were immaculate.

'Wait there, Simon— I'll come down,' she told him, anxious to avoid any awkwardness that might develop if he came up to the apartment.

He smiled up at her, the odd angle of the camera distorting his features. 'Hurry up,' he urged. 'I've got a taxi waiting, and I've booked a table for dinner.'

'I'm coming.' She scooped up her velvet jacket, and hurried out to the lift. Simon was in the hall, chatting easily with the porter on duty—recruiting an ally, Rachel surmised drily. He glanced up as she stepped out of the lift, and his eyes smiled as he surveyed her.

'You look fabulous,' he approved warmly.

'Thank you.'

'Why aren't you wearing the fur wrap I bought you?' he enquired, moving behind her to help her with her jacket.

She hesitated. 'I . . . didn't feel like wearing it. It's such a warm evening.' She drew a deep breath. 'As a matter of fact, I don't like wearing it,' she added with determination. 'I told you when you bought it for me that I don't like wearing real fur. It's cruel.'

'Ah.' He laughed, dismissing her point as trivial. He drew her back against him, his warm breath brushing her temple as he held her close. 'I see you're still wearing the earrings I gave you, though,' he taunted with mocking satisfaction.

'I like them,' she responded stiffly. It was the one thing on which they disagreed, her concern for animal welfare—he accused her of being far too sensitive. 'Shall we go?' she suggested, her eyes cool. 'You said you have a table booked.'

'Ah, yes.' He seemed about to put his arm around her, but then he hesitated, registering her distance with a faintly indulgent smile. 'We're going to a new restaurant tonight,' he told her as they walked out to the taxi. 'You'll like it.'

'Will I?' she murmured drily. It was odd that she had never really noticed before how he was inclined to be so high-handed, assuming that she would automatically like whatever he liked. Why should it have suddenly started to get on her nerves tonight?

She allowed him to hand her into the back of the taxi, but they sat in silence as it purred west through the busy London streets. The restaurant he had chosen was in Chelsea, an area already so well-endowed with eating houses of every description that new ones came and went with the unmarked transience of butterflies in summer. This one was very much in the *nouvelle cuisine* style, decorated with lots of bamboo and chintz, and was obviously the current 'in' place to be seen—many of the usual crowd were there.

She took her seat, uncomfortably aware that the fact that they were together was attracting quite a good deal of attention and gossip. 'Couldn't we have gone somewhere a little more private?' she enquired in a quiet voice as the waiter handed her the menu.

Simon smiled at her across the table. 'Well, we can if you really want to,' he conceded reluctantly. 'But you'll find that the food is excellent here—you'll love the *gratin de crabe*. Then I think the *côtelettes d'agneau*—they do them in an absolutely perfect Périgourdine sauce. And if you want a dessert I'd recommend the *terrine du cassis*.'

'*Oui, monsieur*.' The waiter half bowed, and withdrew as the wine waiter took his place.

'I think I'd like a Chablis for a change,' Rachel mused, knowing that Simon was about to order his customary Montrachet. 'And perhaps a nice Graves with the lamb?'

Simon looked a little taken aback, but the wine waiter beamed. 'An excellent choice, *mademoiselle*. We have a Haut-Brion that I think will prove a most harmonious partner to the dish you have chosen.'

'The '78?' enquired Simon.

'Of course, *monsieur*.'

When they were alone again, Simon cast her a faintly quizzical smile. 'Why the sudden decision to switch wines?' he enquired.

'Oh, I just felt like a change,' she returned airily.

He laughed, dangerously close to being patronising. 'Of course. A little variety is always a good thing.'

'Well, you should know,' she responded tartly.

He looked hurt. 'Please don't let's spoil a good meal by quarrelling,' he begged.

'I thought the whole point of this evening was to talk?'

'There's plenty of time.'

She glared at him, irritated by his air of unimpeachable self-assurance. Did he really think that just a few words were going to put everything right between them? 'By the way,' she announced, prompted by a desire to ruffle him, 'Nick Farlowe is giving a house-warming party tonight. I promised that we'd look in.'

His reaction was most satisfactory. *'What?'* He made a gesture of angry dismissal with his hand. 'That——'

'I thought it might be rather amusing,' she went on, playing it light. 'There's bound to be a lot of very interesting people there.'

He hesitated, considering her point. Nick Farlowe's associates covered a very wide spectrum, from show business to high finance. It was exactly the sort of high-profile gathering that Simon found hard to resist—a chance to make contacts, to put together ideas. But he still couldn't quite suppress his dislike of the arrogant cockney millionaire.

'I don't like the way he looks at you,' he growled. 'If he thinks he's going to get his hands on you...'

She managed a careless laugh. 'Don't be silly, Simon,' she protested, hoping he wouldn't notice the slight tremor in her voice. 'He's very good-looking, of course, I won't deny that. And he makes me laugh. But he really isn't my type— and I'm sure I'm not his.'

'He hasn't got a type. Anything with the right apparatus will do.'

She felt her cheeks tinge faintly pink. 'Don't be crude,' she protested sharply. 'I like him—but just as a friend.'

He seemed to accept her assertion at face-value. 'Very well,' he conceded, smiling. 'If you really want to go to this party, I suppose we could give it half an hour.'

'I'm sure that'll be quite enough,' she agreed readily. She didn't really want to stay longer—she didn't quite trust her own wayward emotions.

Simon nodded, and smoothly changed the subject. 'So,' he enquired. 'How was your trip to Glyndebourne?'

'Oh, it went very well,' she responded, glad to be able to put Nick Farlowe out of her mind for the time being. 'Maria Ewing was on brilliant form.'

He smiled warmly. 'Ah, yes. La Ewing in full flow is quite an impressive sight. Her *Carmen* at Earl's Court Arena was one of the most magnificent things I've ever heard.'

At last Rachel began to allow herself to relax a little. She had always enjoyed Simon's company—he was an interesting and amusing conversationalist, and they really did think alike on so many things. And besides, she couldn't deny that he had a certain style and charisma that were drawing interested glances from several of the other women in the restaurant.

The food was excellent—she had to approve Simon's choice—and as they ate they discussed the current season of operas at Glyndebourne, and then ranged on over the latest production at Covent Garden, and a new exhibition of contemporary paintings at the National Gallery.

But she wasn't prepared to lower her defences just yet. She could enjoy this one evening with him, and afterwards... well, she wasn't going to commit herself. She would just take it one day at a time. Even if they *did* decide to go ahead and get married after all, there was no reason why they should do it on the date they had originally planned.

It was late when they left the restaurant. Simon slanted her a sardonic smile as he hailed a taxi. 'Do you really want to go to this party?' he enquired drily.

Rachel hesitated. She wasn't sure that she did want to go—the thought of seeing Nick made her a little nervous. But that was just silly—she had to face him sooner or later. He was just...a rather attractive man, and she had let him kiss her once—by mistake. It hadn't been important.

'Oh, just for a little while,' she responded lightly. 'We needn't stay—just long enough to be polite.'

'All right,' he conceded, his wry tone conveying his poor opinion of their host. 'Whatever you say.'

A taxi drew up at the kerb, and he handed her into it with all his customary gallantry. But as he climbed in beside her, he seemed about to put his arm around her, and she eased slightly away from him.

His eyes glittered in the darkness. 'What's wrong?' he enquired, a trace of sardonic humour in his voice. 'You're being very defensive.'

'Don't you think I have reason to be?' she countered tersely.

'Oh, Rache.' He reached out and took her hand, gripping it firmly as she tried to draw it away. 'Can't we put that behind us?' he coaxed. 'Believe me, it will never happen again. I love you—you know that.'

She hesitated, gazing down at his hand holding hers. *Could* she learn to trust him again? Marriage to him had seemed to have so much to offer; she had seen a future of happiness and security. And children—she so much wanted children. The contrast of a future alone seemed bleak. She was thirty-one years old now—the years were slipping away. It wasn't very likely that she would meet anyone else...

Into her mind, with sudden vivid clarity, rose the memory of Nick Farlowe's handsome, mocking face, and her lips felt warm with the memory of his kiss. Her heart thudded and began to beat faster as with every ounce of her will she struggled to force the image away. It was laughable to think of Nick in terms of security and a long-term relationship—he just wasn't the kind.

But as Simon slipped his arm around her shoulder, and drew her closer against him, she stiffened. 'Please, Rache. We had a good thing together,' he murmured, fighting her resistance. 'Don't throw it all away. I know I was in the wrong, but I never meant to hurt you. Linda never meant a thing to me.' He put his hand beneath her chin, tilting up her face. 'I could never love anyone but you,' he vowed, his voice husky with sincerity. 'You're so beautiful...'

His head bent towards her, and a surge of panic rose inside her. She had always enjoyed Simon's kisses before, but if she were to find herself drawing a comparison with Nick's... Afraid of facing the implications of that, she turned her head aside quickly, and his lips brushed harmlessly across her cheek.

'No, I...' She drew in a steadying breath, struggling to sort out the turmoil of doubts and questions in her mind. 'I'm sorry, Simon. I...I just need a little more time,' she temporised, the guilt twisting like a knife in her heart. 'Can't you understand that?'

A flicker of impatience crossed his face. 'You know, you're really making a mountain out of a molehill,' he sighed wearily.

She returned him a frosty look. 'It didn't seem like a molehill to me,' she retorted.

'Oh, Rache...' He laughed, catching at her wrist, drawing her inexorably back to him. 'Don't let's start quarrelling about it. Why don't we just

ring everyone and tell them the wedding's back
on?'

'Simon, please...' She twisted her wrist, trying
to break free of him. To her relief, at that
moment the taxi drew to a halt outside the
apartment block, and the driver turned round—
he must have seen the last brief exchange in his
rear-view mirrow, and he didn't seem to like it.

'You OK, miss?' he queried, his eyes
suspicious.

'Oh ... yes, fine, thank you,' she assured him
quickly.

Simon had no choice but to let her go. He paid
off the fare, and helped her out of the taxi. She
found her card-key, but as they walked across
the cobbled courtyard the uniformed security
man on duty recognised her, and pressed the
button on his console desk to open the wide glass
doors.

'Good evening, Miss Haston,' he greeted her
politely.

'Hello, Tom. How's your little girl's chicken-
pox?'

He grinned. 'Much better, thanks, miss. The
spots have gone now, and she's getting a bit
bored, to be honest. Never thought I'd see the
day she was pleading to be allowed to go back
to school!'

Rachel smiled, following Simon into the lift.
He drew her arm possessively through his, but
they didn't speak as they rode up smoothly to the
top floor. She could feel an odd little knot of

tension growing inside her—maybe seeing the two
men side by side would help her sort out the confusion in her mind.

Though really, why there should be any confusion she couldn't understand. She loved Simon,
and it was just a question of whether or not she
could feel able to trust him enough to marry him.
Nick was just a side issue—the reaction she had
felt with him was a purely physical thing, with
no substance to it at all. And even if her feelings
for him *were* stronger than that, his certainly
weren't—she hadn't needed Simon to remind her
of his reputation. It would be a relationship with
no future in it at all.

The lift doors opened, and at once they were
surrounded by the sound of loud rock music,
spilling from the open door of the penthouse.
No wonder Nick had been compelled to invite all
his neighbours, she reflected wryly—otherwise
he might have expected to receive a number of
complaints.

There were a lot of people in the apartment,
but it was so large that it didn't seem at all
crowded. Simon glanced around, a cynical smile
curving his mouth. 'Very nice,' he accorded drily.

Rachel could only echo his approval. It really
was a fabulous apartment. The subtle effects of
well-placed lighting had created pools of intimacy that overcame the impression of being lost
in the vast space, and the glass panels that led
out on to the roof-terrace stood open, inviting
the soft evening air into the room.

She handed her velvet jacket to a polite minion whose smart dark green livery identified him as an employee of one of the top catering firms in the city, accepted a glass of champagne from another, and allowed Simon to draw her hand through his arm and lead her on a tour of critical inspection around the room.

'He's got an eye for a good investment,' conceded Simon grudgingly, examining an intricate construction of black-enamelled metal. 'This is a Murray.'

Rachel had already recognised the work of the fashionable sculptor—there were several more of his pieces in the room. Her own eye had been caught by a painting on the wall. It was by Monet, of the part of the Thames where they now stood, painted on a misty dawn, the blue-grey water reflecting the pale yellow light, so perfectly captured on the canvas that it seemed to touch the pure spirit of the river.

'That's worth a few quid as well,' commented Simon between his teeth.

Rachel flickered him a glance of resentment—with a painting so beautiful, she hated to be reminded of the harsh factor of economics that largely governed the art world.

They threaded their way through the throng; Rachel had not underestimated in her expectation that there would be a lot of interesting people there—had she been an autograph hunter, she could have filled a book. Out on the roof-garden couples were dancing amid the tubs of colourful flowers, and beyond the City tower-blocks traced geometric patterns of light against the night sky, reflecting like diamonds in the shimmering black water of the river. It felt almost as if they were on the top deck of some luxurious liner, moored right here in the Thames.

Rachel glanced around for their host, and smiled wryly to herself as she spotted him across the room, surrounded by an adoring flirtation of women. His tastes seemed quite eclectic—there was the dewy innocence of a girl who looked no older than seventeen, a famous comedienne who was usually noted for her razor-sharp feminism, a sophisticated actress now on the far side of forty. All seemed equally ensnared by that strange magic of his.

He was looking good, as usual, casually dressed in a pair of faded denim jeans that were moulded to his athletic body, and a blue and white shirt, open at the throat, the cuffs rolled back over strong brown wrists. Once again she was forcibly struck by that air of arrant maleness he radiated without any apparent effort.

Catching Rachel's eye over the heads of his fan club, he flashed her one of those devastating smiles, and, ignoring the pouting protests that followed him, he strolled over to greet her.

'Hi, princess. Glad you decided to come.' Those blue-grey eyes swept down over her in undisguised approval. 'You're looking sensational.'

'Thank you,' she managed stiffly. He had completely ignored Simon, who beside her was exuding waves of hostility. She felt a surge of annoyance with both of them—they were like two dogs, growling at each other over a bone. 'Oh, by the way,' she added pointedly, 'you remember Simon Chandler?'

'Of course.' Nick extended a genial hand, but the glint of mocking challenge in his eyes needed no interpretation.

'Good evening,' Simon grated, accepting the briefest handshake and then sliding a possessive arm around Rachel's shoulders. 'Come along, Rache—let's dance,' he suggested tersely.

She acceded without demur, unsettled by the way it made her feel to be caught between the two of them. As they moved away, she cast a flickering glance back over her shoulder at Nick. He caught her eye again, and slanted her a taunting smile, as if he knew exactly how much he disturbed her.

Damn his arrogance. Did he think that just because he had let him kiss her once she was going to throw aside everything she had with Simon, and become another one of his easy conquests? He'd soon find out his mistake! Tilting her head with haughty disdain, she turned away from him.

Simon drew her into his arms and began to dance slowly to the music. She could sense the anger in him, though it was well controlled. 'Well, so you're trying to make me jealous,' he jeered mockingly. 'It isn't going to work, Rache.'

'I don't know what you mean,' she responded, her voice tense with the effort of trying to maintain a semblance of composure.

'I think you do.' His dark eyes glittered down into hers. 'Let me warn you, I'm not the man to play those sort of games with. If you want him, I'll let you go. Go on.' He nodded his head towards where Nick was once again surrounded by his adoring throng of lovely girls. 'He's nothing but a playboy,' he sneered with contempt. 'You'd be just another notch on his belt.'

She could feel her cheeks flushing pink. 'Don't be ridiculous,' she protested. 'I told you, he isn't my type.'

He wasn't—he definitely wasn't. Then why did a casual shirt and jeans seem suddenly so very attractive, when she had always much preferred the sophisticated elegance of a formal dinner-jacket? She could feel herself beginning to panic. Of course it was no more than a physical reaction—he seemed to have the same effect on most of the female gender. But if she didn't find a way to get it under control, and quickly, it could put at risk any chance she might have of a reconciliation with Simon.

But Simon seemed unaware of her agitation. He had bent his head over hers, so that his warm breath was fanning her cheek. 'All right, I believe you,' he laughed softly. 'You've far too much discrimination to fall for a cheap Lothario like that.' He drew her even closer against him.

'Besides, I wouldn't really let you go,' he added possessively. 'You belong to me.'

He was right—he was always right. She closed her eyes, leaning her forehead against his shoulder, letting him wrap her up in his arms. Simon was strong and safe—he would always take care of her. That silly business with Linda...it had probably been her own fault. It must have been a terrible strain on a red-blooded man like Simon to remain celibate for so long. She could hardly blame him—she had found that she was just as susceptible herself to a fleeting spark of attraction for someone else. It was probably just pre-wedding nerves.

From the shelter of his arms, she stole another secret glance at Nick. He was dancing with a willowy blonde, and laughing at something she was saying. Maybe it was because he *was* so different from Simon that she had been attracted to him.

The two men were totally opposite—Simon was hard-working and ambitious, while Nick...well, a large element of luck seemed to have played a substantial part in helping him amass his millions. He didn't seem to take anything seriously—life was just a game to him.

Suddenly Simon's head jerked up. 'Hey, look who's here!' he exclaimed, a note of pleasure in his voice. He took her hand, and drew her across the room. 'Bill—hi, how are you? You remember my fiancée, Rachel Haston?'

Rachel found herself being greeted by someone she vaguely knew—some friend of Simon's, a newspaper editor. She responded politely, though inside she felt a faint stirring of resentment at the distraction. She was introduced to several other men in the group, and their wives, and as she always did when surrounded by strangers she switched on her automatic smile, withdrawing into herself and letting the 'Rachel Haston' persona take over.

'We were just discussing the Government's latest White Paper,' Bill remarked to Simon. 'What do you make of it?'

'Oh, I don't think it'll have a very drastic affect on us in television,' Simon responded seriously. 'It really only consolidates a mish-mash of existing legislation...'

Rachel accepted another glass of champagne from a passing waiter, and sipped it slowly. Simon seemed to have half forgotten her existence—once he began talking politics he could be absorbed for hours. She responded to a few conventional remarks from the wives, but they all seemed to know each other and were busy gossiping about someone she didn't know.

She felt excluded—that familiar sense of detachment, of isolation, was creeping over her. Absently she let her eyes wander along the wall to where the Monet hung. It was such a lovely thing. She had always been drawn to the Impressionists, especially their city-scapes...

'Nice, isn't it?'

She caught her breath as Nick moved up close beside her, so close that she could feel a prickle of tension run over her skin. 'Yes... Yes, it is,' she responded a little unsteadily, taking a small step away from him.

'He's really caught the way the light turns at that time of the morning,' he went on musingly, regarding the painting. She glanced at him, surprised by his unexpected sensitivity, and he lifted one quizzical eyebrow. 'What's wrong?' he enquired, faintly mocking. 'Didn't you think that a grubby working-class cockney could appreciate fine art?'

She blinked, slightly taken aback. Did he think she was a *snob*? Or was he just trying to provoke her again? She tilted her chin at a haughty angle. 'You can hardly claim to be working class,' she countered, letting her gaze drift significantly around the expensive apartment. 'Not any more.'

'No,' he conceded, that taunting smile still curving his arrogant mouth. 'But I started out by getting my hands dirty. And for all your fine, haughty ways you can't quite resist that little bit of curiosity, can you? You wonder what it would be like to go down-market for a change?'

She had to swallow hard, her heart fluttering in a fever. He was wrong that she thought of him as 'down-market'—she had never even considered it—but he was right about that irresistible curiosity. That one kiss had stirred something inside her that she hadn't known was there. What would it be like to lie in his arms, to feel those strong, sure hands caressing her body...?

He seemed to be reading her mind. 'Where's the boyfriend got to?' he enquired, a low, conspiratorial note in his voice.

'Oh, he's...talking business.' She made a vague gesture with her hand towards the corner where Simon was deep in debate.

'Ah.' His eyes glinted with satisfaction. 'Well, he seems fully occupied for the time being, so...'

He drew her into his arms before she could protest, and began to move her to the music. Her first instinct was to pull away from him, but with the slightest tautening of his hard muscles he warned her that he was not going to let her go without a fight. She slanted him a wary glance.

'Relax,' he coaxed, his voice softly mocking. 'What harm can there be in one dance?'

It took every ounce of will-power she possessed to resist the lure of seduction in that voice. 'I...I'm not accustomed to being manhandled,' she responded stiffly.

'Manhandled?' His subtle shift of emphasis somehow changed the meaning of the word entirely. 'No, I don't suppose you are. You look as if you've never been touched. Ice-cool. But we both know that's a false impression, don't we?' He was smiling, a slow, intimate smile that made her feel weak, and his hand began to slide down the length of her back to mould intimately over the base of her spine, holding her far too close for modesty. 'You don't kiss as if you're ice-cool,' he murmured, his warm breath fanning her cheek. 'And your body doesn't feel cool at all at the moment—it feels warm and soft and inviting.'

His words sent a shimmer of heat through her veins. Was this how he had earned his reputation? That low, husky voice was weaving a spell around her, hypnotising her. His cheek was resting against her hair, and she closed her eyes, breathing the evocative musky scent of his skin. The music was slow and sensual, and they were dancing so close . . . it was almost as if they were making love.

She became aware that they had moved out on to the roof-garden. There were few couples out here, and they were all too intensely involved with each other to notice anyone else. The night was dark and romantic, the air filled with the delicate fragrance of the jasmine and honeysuckle that grew in the pots against the wall. The lights that Nick had rigged nestled among the foliage, shedding a soft glow.

There was just a slight breeze, and overhead the sky was like a velvet cloak, spangled with stars—it was a perfect summer evening, high up here above the roofs of London. In the distance, the great bell of Big Ben was solemnly tolling midnight, the sound drifting lazily along the river.

The memory of the way he had kissed her was haunting her mind. That sizzling intensity—had it been only an illusion, or would she feel it again if he kissed her now? Simon was forgotten—she was conscious only of these strong arms around her, the warmth of Nick's breath stirring her hair. The music was low and haunting, the sound of a tenor saxophone drifting around them like blue smoke. It was a night of magic, a night of romance...

A touch on her arm broke into the dream. 'If you're *quite* ready...' Simon grated impatiently.

She blinked up at him, her mind spinning in bewilderment as she struggled to reorientate herself to reality. 'I beg your pardon?' she gasped breathlessly.

'I'm leaving now.'

A sudden surge of anger rose inside her. How *dared* he take her for granted like that? If he hadn't ignored her, so bound up with his fascinating discussion... And after casually introducing her as his fiancée, too, just as if everything had been resolved between them. 'Oh, are you?' she returned coldly. 'Well, I'm not.'

An answering anger flared in his brown eyes. 'Oh? I suppose you'd rather stay here with *him*?' he sneered, nodding with disdain towards Nick, who was watching the exchange with undisguised amusement.

'I'm certainly not running after you when you whistle, like a tame poodle,' she snapped back.

His fingers curled around her arm in a vice-like grip. 'Don't make a scene, Rache,' he warned, a low note of menace in his voice. 'It's customary for a *lady* to leave a party with the man she came with.'

'But the lady doesn't seem to want to leave with you,' Nick put in with the air of one who enjoyed stirring troubled waters.

'You stay out of this,' threatened Simon, his fist clenching.

Nick laughed in scorn. 'I'd let you try it, if it weren't the height of bad manners for a host to start brawling with one of his guests,' he taunted.

'I don't need any lessons in manners from you,' Simon fumed, dangerously close to losing his cool. 'Rache, are you coming or not?'

'No, I am not,' she enunciated clearly. She was painfully aware that the contretemps was attracting a fair amount of attention around them, but she held her head proudly erect, consciously trying to subdue the mortifying blush that was suffusing her cheeks.

'Very well,' conceded Simon tersely. 'Goodnight.' He turned on his heel and walked away without another word. The throng of guests parted like the Red Sea to let him pass.

# CHAPTER FOUR

Rachel became aware that she was shaking. 'I think I'd better take you home,' suggested Nick quietly, sliding a supporting arm around her waist.

'Oh ... yes, thank you,' she agreed, her voice unsteady. Tears were stinging the backs of her eyes—tears of pure, burning anger, but if she let them fall she would look a complete idiot. She let Nick cleave a path for them through the crowded rooms, and out into the comparative quiet of the hallway, collecting her jacket from the waiter as she passed.

Nick pressed the button to summon the lift, and leaned against the wall, watching her as she struggled to compose herself. 'Don't cry over him,' he advised drily. 'He's not worth it.'

'I'm not crying,' she insisted, blinking back the tears. 'At least, not because I'm upset. I'm just so bloody angry!'

He laughed. 'Good for you,' he approved. 'You've every right to be.'

'He really thought I'd just stand there like ... like some potted palm, until he felt like noticing my existence again.' The lift arrived, and he followed her into it. 'I could scream—or kick something. In fact I wish I'd kicked *him*—he deserved it.'

'Remind me never to cross you,' he murmured, a smile lurking in the depths of those blue-grey eyes.

'He's so... arrogant! He treats me as if I don't have any mind of my own. Do you know, whenever he takes me out to dinner, *he* chooses what I want to eat!'

He looked faintly surprised. 'Why do you let him?' he enquired.

'I don't know,' she confessed, laughing at herself. 'Somehow it never bothered me before— I barely even noticed he was doing it. But tonight it really got on my nerves. I felt like just standing up, and walking out on him there and then!'

'That would certainly have got the message home,' he agreed cordially, following her from the lift into her apartment.

'He's always been like that—he's never really listened to a word I had to say, never given my opinions one shred of value.'

'Coffee?'

'What...? Oh, yes, please.' She plumped down on the long leather settee. '*And* he just assumed that I'd be willing to forget all about him and Linda, and go ahead with the wedding as if nothing had happened! I suppose it was my own fault—I should never have agreed to have dinner with him.'

'Why did you?' Nick enquired from the kitchen, where he was busily opening cupboards to find the things to make the coffee.

She felt her cheeks flush faintly pink. He must be thinking she was pathetically stupid. 'Oh, I...I just didn't want to part on bad terms,' she stumbled. 'I thought the least we could do was try to end it as friends.'

'An excellent objective,' he conceded. 'But it doesn't very often work out in practice.'

'No. Well, at least now I know for sure that I really did the right thing in breaking it off with him. It would never have worked out. He's just so sure of his own opinions—I think he would have started to drive me crazy.'

'So you're not in love with him any more?' he enquired, bringing the coffee-cups from the kitchen. He set them down on a low glass table, and settled himself on one of the elegant Italian leather armchairs, watching her steadily as he waited for her response.

The blush in her cheeks deepened to scarlet. How could she answer a question like that, with him sitting there so close? 'I...I don't know,' she stammered, avoiding his eyes. Agitated, she rose to her feet, going over to the window to draw across the slats of the blind, noticing that there was a yellowing leaf to pull off the gloxinia, wandering to the breakfast bar to tidy the rack of coffee-cups.

Had she ever really been in love with Simon? He had never made her feel the way Nick made her feel—trembly and excited, her whole body attuned. Was *this* love—or was it merely physical attraction? Whatever it was, it was entirely new to her, and totally contrary to everything she had ever believed about herself.

Nick was still sitting there, watching her with that slight smile in his eyes, as if he was amused by her aimless fidgeting. 'I don't think you are in love with him any more,' he murmured softly. 'Otherwise you wouldn't look at me the way you do.'

He rose to his feet and came towards her, very slowly. She stared at him, held prisoner by the power of those hypnotic blue eyes. Her heart was pounding so loudly she was afraid he would hear it.

'Such a classy bird,' he murmured, that low, smoky voice infiltrating her defences. He put up one hand, and brushed the backs of his fingers lightly over her cheek. 'You'd be wasted on him.' He leaned towards her, and his mouth brushed over hers, sizzling hot. Her breath caught in her throat, and her lips parted hungrily in anticipation of his kiss.

But instead he drew back, his eyes glinting with mocking humour. 'And if I don't get back upstairs pretty soon, we'll find ourselves in the gossip pages on Monday,' he added teasingly. 'Goodnight, princess.'

She stared at him, stunned with disbelief. He had almost seduced her, and now he was just going to walk away and leave her cold! As the door closed behind him she came abruptly to her senses. She was shaking—with anger, with reaction—and her legs felt so weak that she had to sit down.

Of all the arrogant... He had deliberately made a fool of her, stirring her up with a look, a smile—he obviously thought that he could just snap his fingers whenever it suited him, and she would fall into his arms. Well, he had another think coming! She wasn't like those stupid bimbos who had flocked around him upstairs— she had a little self-respect.

Men—they were nothing but trouble. She had been better off putting all her energies into her career. Well, from now on, that was exactly what she would do. No more Simon, with his high-handed patronising, doing her thinking for her. No more Nick, with his hot kisses and dangerous smile. It was back to ice-cool, untouchable Rachel Haston. At least then she would know exactly where she stood.

It must have been sheer exhaustion after all the emotional turmoil of the evening, but she slept much better than she had expected, and didn't wake till late the following morning. She lay in bed, an echo of some languorous dream still filling her mind, as slowly she became aware that it had been the insistent buzz of the telephone that had woken her. Simon, ringing to apologise? Sleepily she leaned over and picked up the receiver.

'Hi, princess.' That warm, husky voice startled her. She hadn't been expecting Nick to phone, after the way he had left her last night.

'Oh...hello,' she responded a little unsteadily, rolling over on to her stomach.

'Still in bed?' he enquired, the teasingly sensual note in his voice stirring vivid memories of dancing in his arms.

'Y...yes,' she conceded carefully, glad that he couldn't see the blush that had coloured her cheeks.

'So am I,' he murmured. 'Don't you wish you were up here with me?'

She would have liked to have returned him a crisp put-down, but she couldn't think of a thing to say.

'What are you wearing?' he asked wickedly. 'Don't tell me—let me imagine. A soft, clinging silk nightdress—white, I think, and shimmering like an iceberg. Wtih a deep plunge of lace——'

'Hey, what is this?' she protested, laughing in spite of herself as she struggled to pull herself together. 'Don't you think heavy breathing at this time on a Sunday morning is a little indecent?'

He laughed softly. 'Not at all—it's the nicest way to start the day. Almost the nicest,' he corrected himself, the velvet timbre of his voice caressing her. 'It would be even better if you were up here with me.'

His words were making her heartbeat race so fast she felt dizzy. 'No, I...I don't think so,' she managed to respond.

'Don't you? I think it would be an excellent idea,' he murmured huskily. 'One of my best. Why don't you come on up and let me prove it to you?'

She closed her eyes as her own treacherous imagination filled her head with the thought of lying in bed with him. She turned over on to her back, her body aching with a strange hunger.

*No*—this was crazy. Forcefully dispelling the images from her mind, she sat up. 'I dare say it would be fun for a while,' she responded, crisply dismissive. 'But I'm afraid casual sex doesn't really interest me.'

'What do you want, princess?' he taunted with dry cynicism. 'Diamond rings and wedding bells, and a guy who brings you red roses?'

'What's wrong with that?' she countered with dignity.

'Nothing, I dare say,' he drawled laconically. 'But you can count me out—I'm not the permanent kind.'

He didn't need to tell her that—she already knew. So why did it hurt so much to hear him say it? 'Was there any other reason for this phone call, apart from trying to guess what I wear in bed?' she enquired, injecting a note of cool indifference into her voice.

'How do you fancy a nice rowdy afternoon, knee-deep in mud, and a nice greasy hot dog to keep you warm?' he enquired, a hint of mocking challenge in his voice. 'Or is scramble-racing beneath the dignity of the sophisticated Rachel Haston?'

'Of course not,' she protested, stung.

'Good. I'll be down in twenty minutes,' he said, and hung up before she could argue.

She stared blankly at the receiver. Why on earth had she let him trick her into agreeing to go out with him? The last thing she wanted was to spend an entire afternoon with him. And yet... after all, what possible harm could there be in it? It would be broad daylight, there would be plenty of people around...

And besides, she had no intention of waiting around home in case Simon decided to call with an apology for his behaviour last night. As far as she was concerned, that relationship was over. So why shouldn't she go out with Nick? She was a free agent. So long as she was very careful not to lose her head...

Scramble-racing, of all things! It was hardly the way she would have chosen to spend a Sunday afternoon. But he had made it sound like such fun. She swung herself out of bed, buoyed up by a thrill of exhilaration that she didn't want to examine too closely.

She was ready by the time Nick knocked on her door. Mindful of his warning about the mud, she had dressed with casual smartness in a pair of figure-hugging designer jeans, tucked into the top of a pair of tan leather boots, and a loose white T-shirt knotted around her hips. Her hair was tied up in a twist on the crown of her head with a length of white ribbon. Scooping up her pink ski-jacket, she went to let him in.

Those blue-grey eyes slid down over her in an undisguised appreciation that set her pulse racing. 'Mmm—you look sensational,' he approved, smiling that irresistible smile. 'What was it we were supposed to be doing this afternoon?'

'Scramble-racing,' she responded, laughing unsteadily.

'Oh, yes.' He pulled a face of playful reluctance. 'I suppose we'd better be going, then. And behave yourself—there'll be a couple of hundred people there, and with you looking like that the slightest provocation is likely to make me forget myself and throw you right down in the grass.'

'Mud,' she corrected him sweetly.

'Grrr! Even better!' He came after her like a monster, chasing her out of the flat, and catching her in a great bear-hug by the lift, sweeping her up off the ground and making her squeal with laughter. She wriggled in his arms, enjoying the delicious sensation of moving her body against his.

The lift doors opened, and a couple of their most staid neighbours stepped out—a middle-aged couple, he was something in the wine trade. Their shocked reaction was quickly hidden behind a politely smiling mask, but Rachel and Nick collapsed with laughter as they stepped into the lift and the doors closed behind them.

'Oh, dear—did you see her face?' giggled Rachel. 'Anyone would have thought you had your hand up my T-shirt!'

'What an excellent idea,' he teased, pushing her back into a corner.

'Stop it!' she protested, defending herself as best she could, breathless with laughter. The sensation of trying to match her muscles to his much greater strength stirred images in her brain. Images of making love, right here in this lift...

As if he was aware of that too, he drew away from her, his eyes glinting with a knowing smile. She felt a shimmer of apprehension run through her. It seemed that he had agreed to turn the temperature down to simmer—at least for the time being...

The lift reached the basement, and as they stepped out he offered her his hand. She put hers in it, her heart skipping with pleasure. Maybe it *was* no more than a physical attraction—but it made her feel great.

'Ever ridden a motorbike?' he asked as they walked through the underground garage.

'Of course,' she responded promptly. 'My elder brother had one when we were in our teens. I often rode pillion.'

'Good. So you know what to do, then.' He stopped, smiling with pride at the gleaming machine that occupied one of the parking spaces.

'Oh...' Rachel regarded it with some misgiving. It was rather a different proposition from her brother's old grease-box. This one was big—

the engine looked as big as a car's engine beneath the black leather seat.

'Nice, isn't it?' enquired Nick, opening the baggage-trunk concealed within the streamlined fibreglass faring, and handing her a black crash-helmet.

'Er... I'm not sure if that's the word I'd use,' she murmured uncertainly.

'Best bike on the road,' he assured her. 'It's a Norton. I'll tell you, once you've driven one of these you'll never go back to a car—not in London.'

'I'm sure it's very practical,' she mused, surveying the bike's powerful lines with a degree of doubt.

'Don't worry,' he assured her. 'Just wrap your arms around me, hang on tight, and move as it goes.' The husky tone of his voice teasingly implied he wasn't just talking about riding the big motorbike.

He lowered his own helmet over his head, the dark visor hiding his face. Rachel stared up at him. Without those laughing blue-grey eyes, suddenly he was a stranger again—rather a frightening one. What did she really know about this man? Virtually nothing, except what she had read in the papers. Was it really wise to go off for the whole afternoon with him?

He swung one long leg over the bike, and the engine sprang to life with a full-throated roar that echoed around the cool stone vaults of the underground car park. Rachel hesitated, afraid of both bike and rider. Both were more powerful, more dangerous, than anything she was used to, and an instinct of self-preservation warned her to turn around and go straight back upstairs to the safety of her own self-contained little white-walled flat.

But he had pulled the bike back off its rests, and turned it round, and now he was waiting for her to get on. And the strange fascination he held for her was even stronger than her fear. She wanted to spend the afternoon with him—and the price was to step on to this bike. Swallowing hard, she pulled the helmet down over her head, and swung her leg across the saddle.

The surge of power seemed to thrill right through her body. She had one last moment to change her mind, as they paused at the exit to the car park to wait for the security barrier to open, and then they were sweeping out into the bright sunlight and the traffic.

They were flying, smooth and fast—the fear was still there, like spice, adding a piquancy to the most exhilarating feeling she had ever experienced. She leaned against Nick's wide back, her arms tight around his waist, feeling as though they and the bike were one single unit, fused in a miracle of balance and speed.

It was . . . almost like making love. Helplessly she fought to shake the erotic imagery from her mind, but it was too powerful. Nick Farlowe had bewitched her, turning her into some fierce, sensual creature which she didn't recognise. She closed her eyes, and let her thoughts drift in some wild, uncharted land where no inhibitions bounded the limits of her imagination.

They didn't have far to go. As they turned off the Mile End Road and drove down a street of brown terraced houses, they came up to and overtook a travelling camper plastered with stickers, and then a dusty old estate car with two scramble-bikes on a trailer. Nick peeped his horn, and the drivers waved, apparently in recognition.

A left turn, and under an old railway bridge, and they came to a wide open space of derelict land, where there were already quite a lot of people gathered. Smoothly negotiating the pot-holes, Nick parked the big bike among a row of cars.

It was like a fairground. There were more motorbikes than Rachel had ever seen in one place, trailers and caravans, and a hot-dog truck already doing a brisk trade. She pulled off her crash-helmet, and gazed around, fascinated.

'Nick!' A tall, chunkily built black man in oily overalls came striding over, greeting him with a cheerful slap of hands. 'How you doing, man?'

'Not so bad, old son. Yourself?' Nick took Rachel's crash-helmet, and put it with his in the trunk of the bike. 'Rachel, this is Big Jim Bradley. Jim, Rachel Haston.'

The big man smiled broadly in welcome, offering her his huge hand. 'Hello,' he said. 'Very pleased to meet you.' It seemed that he genuinely was, as well, though it was evident that he hadn't recognised her. Such open friendliness was unfamiliar to her—so different from the kind of superficial gloss of affection that passed for warmth in her world.

'How do you do?' she responded, warming to him as his strong fingers closed gently around hers.

'I hope he's warned you it's going to be muddy?' he enquired, nodding his head in Nick's direction.

'Yes, he did. But it shouldn't be too bad, should it? It's such a lovely sunny day.'

He chuckled. 'Ah, but they hose down the course,' he told her, pointing towards the track. It was glistening wetly, and a man was still standing by it, playing water over it from a garden hose. 'Otherwise it rips up all the dust, see, and that gets in the bikes.'

She smiled wryly, glancing down at her clothes—maybe they weren't quite as suitable as she had thought they would be, but she didn't really have any of her 'country' clothes with her in London. 'Oh, well, never mind,' she sighed. 'I suppose mud's easy enough to wash out.'

He boomed with laughter. 'You'll do!' he approved roundly.

Suddenly a whole bunch of kids were converging around them, clamouring for Nick's attention.

'Barry's got the fastest time in practice, Nick!'

'Where do you reckon's the best place on the line up, Nick? Out to the right?'

'Have you seen the new DR the Mercurys have got? It's really ace, man. Got a Mikuni flatside carburettor, and the suspension's brilliant!'

Nick grinned at Rachel over their heads, and Big Jim chuckled at her bemused expression. 'This is the club,' he told her. 'Farlowe's Falcons, they call themselves—picked the name themselves.' He obviously found their choice highly amusing.

She was still puzzled. 'Why Farlowe's Falcons?' she asked.

'Nick sponsors them, see. Got them the lease on this scratch of ground, pays for the bikes— these kids could never afford their own, not in a month of Sundays. They think he's the greatest thing since sliced bread.' He was still laughing, but his own respect was evident.

She glanced across at Nick, seeing him with new eyes. It was a surprise to learn that he was a philanthropist—and not just handing out his money to cold charity, but taking an active interest in the welfare of a bunch of kids.

But then it was evident that he enjoyed it. The boys clearly hero-worshipped him, and he seemed happy and relaxed in their company—there was no trace of that sardonic edge in his smile that had been so evident at his party, when he had been surrounded by all those adoring bimbos.

He must have been like these kids himself once, she reflected. A bike-mad city kid, with no money for a bike of his own, and nowhere to ride it if he could have got hold of one. She found herself wondering what sort of childhood he had had. What had driven his compulsion to make himself rich? Where were his family now?

'Come and have a look at the bikes, Nick, and tell us if you think we've got them set up right,' the lads were pleading, hanging on to his arms.

'All right, all right,' he agreed genially. He held out his hand to Rachel, and as she took it she had to smile at the expressions on the faces of the admiring young boys—they clearly didn't approve of his bringing a *girl* along to get in the way.

'What was it you said your brother used to ride?' Nick asked her, drawing her into the conversation.

'Oh, it was an old Triumph. He and my cousin restored it together.'

'A Triumph?' The boys gazed at her with a new respect. 'What sort was it?'

'Oh, a Tiger, I think,' she said vaguely, stretching her brains to remember.

That clearly impressed them. 'Wow! That's a real classic!'

Nick smiled at her. 'You just scored a few points,' he told her. 'Fancy a cup of tea before the racing starts?'

She nodded. 'Yes, please.'

'Come on, then—how about you, Jim?'

They strolled over to the hot-dog truck. Quite a few other people seemed to have had the same idea, but the crowd made way for Nick, all greeting him like old friends. He introduced

Rachel to them, and she soon found herself involved in their conversations, drawn in by their cheerful camaraderie.

Nick kept his arm casually around her waist all the time, and she found herself revelling in a certain pride in being at his side. Here in this man's world he was a king, his opinions sought and respected by all. And all the time she was aware of the hard, muscular strength of his body against hers, of the firm line of his jaw, the way his wiry blond hair curled over his ears. Even as she smiled and chatted, there was an ever-present ache deep inside her, and sometimes when he looked down at her she recognised the same thought in his eyes.

It unnerved her, the way she wanted him. She had never known anything quite like it before, and she wasn't sure that she would be able to keep it under control. But control it she must, she warned herself quickly. It was tempting to let herself believe that it was in some way unique that he had brought her here, into his other world, but the unquestioning way her presence had been accepted told her that it was not at all unusual.

How many other girls had stood here drinking this powerful brown brew of tea, had revelled in the casual intimacy of that possessive arm around their waists? Was it a trick he used, when his other techniques for undermining a girl's defences were slow to work?

That thought was a little deflating—like a fool, she would have liked to be able to imagine that she was at least a little bit special. Of course, she knew what kind of man he was—at least he had never tried to deceive her that he would take a relationship seriously. And after all, why should he? He was only twenty-nine—it was natural that he would still be playing the field. Any woman who fell in love with him would just be asking for trouble...

A sudden surge of activity warned that it was time for the races to start. The first was to be the small eighty cc bikes, ridden by the younger boys. They were lining up at the start, bouncing with excitement, their parents and older friends bombarding them with advice.

The course was a circuit of about four hundred yards, a dirt track maybe ten yards wide, very uneven, with the most alarming bumps and dips to be negotiated. 'What happens if they fall off?' asked Rachel, leaning close to Nick to be heard above the din of the revving bikes.

'They get back on again,' he responded with a grin. 'Don't worry—they're well padded with body armour, and we teach them how to roll. It's not very often one gets hurt, not when they learn properly through a club. But we've got a first-aid post here, just in case.'

She nodded, watching as the wire went up, and the race began. It was a frantic scramble for position, the bikes bouncing fiercely over the track, sliding almost on their sides around the bends. One of the young Falcons was in second place, and Rachel found herself caught up in the excitement, cheering him on as loudly as Nick beside her.

The youngsters did four laps of the circuit, and the young Falcon held on to his second place, running up eagerly when the race was over for Nick to congratulate him and listen with patient interest to his breathless rerun of the whole event.

It was the most entertaining afternoon Rachel had spent in a long time. If anyone had told her that she would have enjoyed it all so much—the noise, the mud, even the wafting aroma of greasy hot dogs mingling with the sharp smell of petrol—she would have laughed. But it was such a lively change from her usual surroundings—and it was such fun to be with Nick.

By six o'clock, when the last race finished, she had shouted herself almost hoarse, cheering on their Falcons, and she was liberally spattered with mud. Nick glanced down at her, laughing. 'You've got freckles,' he teased gently.

'So have you.' She took a tissue from her bag, and, moistening it with the tip of her tongue, she began wiping the mud-spots from his face. When she had finished he took it from her and returned the favour.

'There, that's better.' Those blue-grey eyes were smiling down into hers, the message in them making her heart skid and begin to race out of control. I want you. Unconciously she put out her hand to steady herself, her fingertips encountering the hard wall of his chest. He put his hand over hers, strong and possessive. It was just too much for her to fight...

'Cheerio, then, Nick!'

The brief moment was shattered by Big Jim's cheerful farewell. Nick turned to wave to him as he drove past, still keeping hold of Rachel's hand. The ground was rapidly clearing, cars and motorbikes streaming away under the railway bridge.

Nick glanced around, a reminiscent smile on his face. 'I used to play over here when I was a kid,' he told her.

'Oh?' She was having to struggle to regain her breath. 'You grew up near here, then?'

'Over there.' He pointed to a group of three ugly blocks of high-rise flats on the far side of the railway line. Drawing her with him, he began to stroll across towards them.

There was a rickety old footbridge across the railway lines. The flats were set in a wide expanse of grass, criss-crossed with trodden paths. As they drew closer she could see the litter and the vandalism that scarred them—ugliness on ugliness, a place that no one would want to bother caring about.

'I lived here with my nan and grandad, up there on the ninth floor,' Nick told her, tipping his head back to stare up at the building. 'That one—see, with the blue balcony.'

'Do they still live there?' she enquired uncertainly.

He looked surprised at her question. 'No. They both died years ago.'

'Oh, I'm sorry.' She gazed down at her feet, desperately wanting to know more about him, but shy of seeming to pry. 'What would you have done—if they were still alive, I mean? Would you have bought them a nice home somewhere now that you're rich, or do you think they wouldn't have wanted to move away?'

He seemed to give this a moment's consideration. 'I don't think they'd have wanted to move far,' he mused. 'Maybe into a nice little house over by the Gardens. They'd lived round here all their lives, you see, and generations of Farlowes before them. They wouldn't have taken to being transplanted, not at their time of life.' He sighed, as if remembering happy times.

'What about your parents?' she asked. 'Where do they live?'

He shrugged. 'Oh, my mum lives up in Tottenham somewhere. She doesn't bother much with me, and I don't bother much with her. I don't know where my father is—he was never married to my mum, and they split up just after I was born. I suppose it must have been pretty tough on her, stuck with a kid, so she dumped me on my nan, and went off.'

She glanced up at him in concern, but there was no trace of bitterness in his eyes.

'I must have been a right little handful,' he recalled, smiling. 'The first time the police brought me home for pinching lead off the church roof I was only seven. Lord, how my nan paled me for that!' He laughed. 'By the third or fourth time, I'd learned my lesson. After that I used to go round with an old pram, knocking on doors for scrap.' He aimed an idle kick at an old tin can lying in the kerb.

'Did you really set out right back then to make yourself a millionaire?' she enquired curiously.

'Not really—I never really thought of it in those terms back then. I just knew it was no fun being poor.' He grinned, and dropped his arm casually around her shoulders. 'Obviously the chap who said money can't buy happiness never had to live on bread and dripping at the end of the week until pay day.'

She smiled up at him. 'Did you?'

'Often. The funny thing is, I still like it. But now, how about some dinner?'

'Bread and dripping?' she teased.

'No!' He laughed, swinging her round to lead her footsteps back towards where they had left the bike. 'I was thinking more along the lines of a nice little Italian restaurant I know, very cosy, does the best lasagne I've ever tasted.'

'Sounds good,' she agreed readily.

'It is.'

CHAPTER FIVE

THE restaurant was a delight. Far from the fashionable areas of the West End, it was blissfully free of the clichés of red and white checked tablecloths and candles stuck in Chianti bottles. The floor and the tables were plain scrubbed wood, and the walls were of white paint over brick, covered with warm, sunny paintings of pretty Tuscan villages.

The place was already quite full—clearly quite a few of the *cognoscenti* had found their way to this Mediterranean corner of Limehouse. The proprietor was busy serving, but he glanced round as they came in, and his face broke into a broad smile. 'Nick! *Ciao*—good to see you! Rosanna?' He raised his voice towards the kitchen. 'Come see who's here.'

An attractive dark-haired woman in a plastic apron appeared in the doorway, and as soon as she saw Nick she hurried forward, throwing her arms around his neck. 'Nick! Where've you been? It's been weeks!'

He laughed, returning the hug. 'No more than three weeks, Rosa,' he argued. 'Besides, if I ate too much of your great cooking I'd end up as fat as your Sandro here.' He patted the Italian's portly figure with affection.

Sandro shook with laughter, and squeezed Nick's shoulders. 'This man is my brother,' he announced to a surprised Rachel.

She stared from one to the other, taking in the contrast of blond hair and black, blue-grey eyes and deep liquid brown. Sandro burst into loud laughter, amused that she should take him literally.

'When I am broke, my restaurant closing down, great fat overdraft and the bank won't lend me no more money, he says to me, "Sandro, your wife cooks the best I ever tasted. It's a crime to let you go out of business." And who am I to argue?' He shrugged generously. 'So, now we are partners. Brothers.'

Nick smiled. 'I still reckon I got the best end of the deal,' he insisted. 'Sandro, Rosa, this is Rachel.'

'Welcome, Rachel.' Sandro took her hand in his two great paws. 'What a delight to meet you. Ah, so beautiful!' He launched into a flood of voluble Italian, the expression in his eyes conveying a thousand compliments.

Rosa laughed, and punched him playfully on the shoulder. 'Stop trying to steal your best friend's girl,' she warned him. 'Rachel, I'm happy to meet you. Have a seat, and see what you'd like to eat.'

Rachel smiled at her. 'I'd really like to tidy myself up a bit first,' she said. 'We've been at a motorbike meeting all afternoon.'

Rosa shuddered with exaggerated sympathy. 'Ah! Don't tell me for motorbikes!' she exclaimed. 'Nasty, noisy things. You let him take you to one of those?' She took her arm, leading her through to the back of the restaurant. 'Here, you go upstairs to the bathroom, have a nice wash—plenty of towels up there, help yourself.'

'Thank you very much.'

A flight of steep stairs led up to a dark landing. The bathroom was the first door on the left—a tiny room, and very old-fashioned, but spotlessly clean. Catching sight of her reflection in the mirror above the sink, Rachel smiled wryly—she looked as if she'd been pulled through a hedge backwards.

As Rosa had promised, there were plenty of towels. She washed her face, and carefully combed the tangles out of her hair, and tied it up neatly again, and then reapplied her make-up with a light hand. Then she stood and gazed thoughtfully at the image of her face in the mirror, a slight frown marring the smooth line of her brow.

Had it been wise to agree to have dinner with him? It hadn't been her intention to let their innocent daytime date linger on into the evening. What was it about that man, that he seemed able to make her do whatever he wanted? She had been acting completely out of character from the moment she had met him.

In her early days in television she had learned deep-breathing exercises to help her relax before

going in front of the cameras—she still used them
occasionally, not entirely immune to nerves.
Closing her eyes, she drew in a long, steady
breath as she counted slowly to four, held it, and
then let it go, very controlled. The effect was very
soothing. She practised it again a few times, until
she felt ready to face anything.

She could hear Nick's laughter in the kitchen
as she descended the stairs. Uncertainly she
paused in the doorway. Delicious smells were
issuing from the pans simmering on the large steel
hob, and Nick was sampling the contents of one
with a spoon, watched eagerly by Rosa and a
younger girl who looked enough like her to be
her sister.

'You like it?' the girl was asking anxiously. 'A
little more *sardo* perhaps?'

He shook his head, smiling down into the up-
turned face. 'No, it's perfect just as it is,' he
assured her.

Rachel felt a sudden twist of jealousy in her
heart. The girl was pretty, with the budding
promise of a lush beauty to come, and he was
smiling at her with that special, intimate smile
that had made her own heart weaken. Did he
smile at every pretty woman he met in that way,
spinning his fraudulent spells around them?

He glanced up and saw her, and that smile
turned itself on her. 'Come and have a taste of
this,' he invited.

She hesitated, mustering every ounce of composure she possessed to counter the treacherous

weakness he engendered inside her. 'What is it?' she enquired, her voice commendably even.

'*Pesto* sauce.' He offered her a spoonful, and she took it, aware of the dark, hostile glitter in the young girl's eyes. 'What do you think?' he asked.

'Very nice,' she approved.

'There, Maria,' he teased. 'You'll soon be as wonderful a cook as your sister.'

'Ah, she has far to go yet,' protested Sandro, bustling into the kitchen. 'But she is young, she has plenty of time, eh, *bambina*?' He pinched the girl's cheek affectionately, but she clearly didn't like being called a child in front of Nick, and her expression was sulky as she turned back to stirring her sauce.

There was a moment of awkwardness as everyone pretended not to notice Maria's behaviour. Then Sandro laughed again. 'So, my friend, you have a good appetite tonight, yes? I have the best table for you, then, and a bottle of my finest Frascati, cool from the cellar.'

He ushered them from the kitchen, and showed them to a table in the corner, holding out a seat for Rachel to sit down. 'Here is the menu. Choose and enjoy.'

He stood by proudly as Rachel commented on the magnificent selection. She decided to start with an *antipasto* of shellfish, followed by the lasagne that Nick had recommended, and promised herself that she would leave room for a zabaglione for dessert.

'They seem very nice people,' she commented to Nick when they were alone. 'How long have you known them?'

'Oh, quite a few years. Would you like some wine?'

'A little, please.'

He filled her glass, and she picked it up, surprised to see that its colour was the delicate pale gold of a good burgundy. Simon had always tended to dismiss Italian wines, preferring the superior French regions of Burgundy and Bordeaux.

She swirled the liquid thoughtfully in her glass, savouring the bouquet. This was a wine of some finesse. Taking a small sip on to her tongue, she drew a breath across it, savouring the harmony of subtle fruitiness and elegant maturity. The smooth flavour lingered long after the wine had gone.

Nick was watching her with a certain cynical amusement. 'Well? Does it meet with your approval?' he enquired drily.

'Yes, it does. Very good indeed.'

'Who taught you to taste wine like that?'

She hesitated, detecting a hint of disapproval in his tone. 'Simon,' she informed him, retreating behind a defensive barrier of cool dignity.

His mouth curved in a sardonic smile. 'And did he teach you to be a snob about it too?'

His words stung. A snob—was that really what he thought of her? 'I don't know why on earth you should want to go out with me if you don't even like me,' she retaliated.

He lifted one eyebrow, genuinely surprised. 'What on earth makes you think I don't like you?' he asked.

'You said I was a stuck-up bitch, a snob...'

He laughed softly, those blue-grey eyes capturing her with their hypnotic gaze. 'You are a snob, in some ways,' he murmured, his voice low and husky. 'But I don't mind that—I shall enjoy taking you down from your pedestal.'

The explicit meaning in his words brought a flush of warmth to her cheeks. She swallowed hard, struggling to regain some composure as Sandro approached their table. He could not miss the tell-tale signs, though his romantic Italian soul misinterpreted them, and he chuckled indulgently.

'Here we are. *Frutti di mare*,' he announced, rolling the words luxuriantly over his tongue. '*Gamberi*—in English is prawns—salt cod, *vongole*. Served in my Rosa's special dresssing.' He kissed his fingertips. 'Enjoy.'

He withdrew, leaving them alone again. Rachel was aware that her cheeks were still faintly flushed with pink, but she kept her eyes lowered as she served a portion of the *antipasto* on to her plate. Her appetite, keened by the afternoon in the fresh air, had vanished.

What was happening to her? She had never felt quite like this before, so totally aware of her own vulnerability. Her numbed brain sought desperately for some neutral topic of conversation, anything to ease the shimmering atmosphere of tension between them.

'Wh-who painted the pictures on the walls?' she asked, her voice sounding oddly strained to her own ears.

'A cousin of Sandro's.'

'Oh.' She struggled for something else to say. 'Do you...do you do this a lot?' she enquired, trying for a light touch of humour. 'Invest in your friends' businesses, I mean.'

'Only the ones I think are genuinely worth it,' he responded, smiling lazily. 'I'm not a soft touch.'

'No.' She could well believe that. 'What sort of things do you invest in?'

'Are you a spy from the Tax Office?' he protested, his eyes dancing with amusement. 'Well, there's a furniture business—did you notice the stuff in my apartment? A good friend of mine made that—real craftsmanship, but that kind of business takes a long time to establish. Not many people can afford the prices that sort of work commands, and reputations grow slowly.'

She nodded, interested.

'Then I've got another friend who's in the recycling business—paper, glass, anything really. He's pioneering a new way of making print-quality paper from re-pulped waste, without using dioxin bleaches. If it works out, he's going to give away the technology free to anyone who wants it.'

Her eyes widened in surprise. 'That's not much of a way to make money,' she commented.

'It isn't about making money,' he returned, surprisingly serious. 'It's about saving the planet. Don't you think that's important?'

'Yes, of course I do. But——'

'But you didn't think I did,' he supplied for her. 'You really think I'm some kind of philistine, don't you?'

'No, I . . .' She smiled, and blushed. 'Yes, I suppose I did,' she confessed awkwardly.

He laughed softly. 'You look gorgeous when you blush,' he teased.

A warm glow seemed to be spreading slowly through her whole body, and some irresistible force compelled her to lift her eyes to his face. He was smiling that fatal smile, and she felt herself melting inside. She looked away again quickly.

Why had she let herself walk into this? She had warned herself last night that he was dangerous. But what could she do? Even here, in this crowded restaurant, just one look from those blue-grey eyes could capture her, could make her feel as though he was already seducing her, as though she was already yielding. How could she ever hope to keep things under control when they were alone?

It was difficult to concentrate on her meal, though the food was excellent—a fact which Sandro accepted as a foregone conclusion when she complimented him on it. 'Of course.' He dropped his plump arm around Nick's shoulders, hugging him with fierce affection. 'With his brains, and my beauty...'

She laughed, hoping he would stay, glad of the brief respite from the strain of being alone with Nick.

Nick was leaning back in his seat, sipping his wine. 'I'm glad you're enjoying it,' he remarked casually. 'Come again, bring some friends—then they'll go away and tell *their* friends about it. That's how word gets around.'

His thoughtless words chilled her. How could he imagine that she would ever be able to come here again without him? But of course he would think like that—he would expect that, if they should have an affair, it would in the natural course of events come to an end, and then life for both of them would resume much as it had before they had met. It would never even occur to him that he could leave her with a broken heart...

'Coffee?'

'What? Oh... Yes, please.'

Those blue-grey eyes were watching her across the table, so perceptive that they seemed to see right through the layers of defence with which she had surrounded herself for so long. But when he spoke, it was on a safely neutral subject. 'How did your brother come by his Tiger?' he asked.

'Oh, he found it rusting in the back of a barn near where we lived,' she told him, managing to speak lightly. 'The farmer didn't want it—he was glad to get it out of his way.' She smiled, reminiscing. 'He lived for that bike, did Richard. My mum used to go mad at him, getting all oily and dirty, but he never took any notice.'

'You lived in the country?'

'Cheshire—well, the outskirts of Manchester really, though my mum would never admit it. Now she really *is* a snob,' she added, laughing awkwardly. 'She even tries to get my dad to drop his Manchester accent—not with a great deal of success. He says he's done well enough talking plain.' Almost unconsciously she had begun to mimick her father's stolid Ancoats burr. 'He's not going to change at his time of life, thank you very much!'

He laughed with her, but suddenly she felt embarrassed. She had given away far too much about herself, things she usually kept secret. But as she tried to withdraw he reached out and took her hand.

'No, don't close up on me again,' he coaxed. 'What are you afraid of?'

She had to fight to resist the warm persuasion in his voice. He was holding her hand in his, stroking his thumb lightly over the delicate veins inside her wrist, where the tumultuous pulses were betraying the effect he was having on her. It was the most erotic sensation she had ever known; her heart was beating so fast she felt dizzy, and her breath was warm on her lips. He had reduced her to a state of utter helplessness—and yet all he was doing was touching her hand.

'I ... Excuse me, I ... I'd better just ... go and comb my hair again before we go home,' she stammered, almost knocking her chair over as she stood up. She fled for the safety of the upstairs bathroom, where she bolted the door and sat down weakly on the edge of the bath.

This was crazy, just totally crazy. She had to get a grip on herself, or she would go insane. That man knew every trick in the book, and then some, and he used them quite mercilessly. She closed her eyes, but the image of his face across the table was still indelibly etched in her brain, and her body was aching as if it had been her naked skin he had been caressing.

Shakily she stood up, and filled the sink with cold water, immersing her hands in it as if to anaesthetise them from the memory of that sensuous touch. Her image in the mirror stared back at her, the eyes wide and dark, the mouth soft with desire.

Beautiful—everybody said she was, and the evidence of her own eyes couldn't be denied. But was that enough? What would it take to make a man like Nick Farlowe want more than just to get her into bed? After tonight, she could no longer pretend that it was just a physical thing— she *was* falling in love with him.

Today she had come to know a different side of him from the one he had let her see before. And she liked the kind of person he was, liked his casual generosity, liked the open friendliness of his manner.

'So now what?' she asked herself with a trace of bitterness. He had made it more than clear that he was offering no commitment. If she let herself surrender to the fatal temptation he held out, she could be very sure that there would be no future in it.

Oh, he wanted her badly enough at the moment, and maybe with careful strategy she could make him want her a little longer. But in the end there would be only heartbreak. And yet . . . she wanted him—so much that it hurt.

With a sigh she bent over the sink, and splashed her face with the cool water. She wouldn't go out with him again. It had been a mistake—a dangerous mistake—but she had learned her lesson. And for tonight . . . well, she was just going to have to do her best to ensure that she didn't let things get out of control. And that was going to take every ounce of will-power she possessed.

Nick was in the kitchen again when she went downstairs, joking with Sandro and flirting with Rosa and Maria as he polished off the remains of a second helping of lemon sorbet. She fixed a bright smile on her face, and crossed to his side.

'Ready to go?' he asked, glancing down at her.

'If you are.'

'Right then. *Ciao*, Sandro.' He suffered the beaming Italian to hug him and kiss both his cheeks, and then he kissed Rosa as Sandro descended on Rachel. As she was swept into a huge brotherly hug, she saw Maria, standing beside her sister, awaiting her turn for a kiss from Nick, her dark eyes sparkling with an intensity that was unmistakable. Rachel tried hard not to take too much notice, turning instead to Rosa.

'Thank you for a lovely meal,' she said warmly. 'It was one of the best I've ever had.'

Rosa dimpled with pleasure. *'Grazie,'* she responded shyly. 'I'm so glad you enjoyed it.*Arrivederci*—goodnight.'

Nick was still deeply involved in a murmured conversation with Maria, his hands resting on her shoulders. Rachel forced herself to continue to smile, and chat to Sandro and Rosa as if there was nothing wrong, but she couldn't suppress the painful twinges of jealousy inside her.

At last he turned back to her, and dropped a casual arm around her shoulders. 'Well, come on, then, princess, let's be going.'

'Fine,' she responded coolly.

He caught the note in her voice at once, and slanted her a searching glance, but he didn't say anything until they were outside. Then he enquired drily, 'OK, what's wrong?'

She tilted her chin at a haughty angle. 'Nothing. Why should there be anything wrong?' she countered, instantly defensive.

He dismissed her denial with a shake of his head. 'The temperature's dropped below zero. There must be a reason.'

'Not at all. I just wouldn't have wanted to drag you away from there before you were *absolutely* ready.'

'Ah!' He smiled knowingly. 'Do I detect the faintest hint of jealousy?'

'Of course not!'

He laughed softly, drawing her close. 'You shouldn't mind Maria,' he told her. 'She's been in love with me since she was about three years old. I admit she's going to be gorgeous, but my taste runs to cool, elegant blondes.'

In the middle of the street his arms were around her, and she could feel the warning tension of male arousal in him. She stared up at him, frightened by the intensity of need inside her. It was a fire that threatened to consume her, leaving nothing but ashes.

In an instinct of pure self-preservation she closed her eyes, struggling to resist the almost overwhelming temptation to let herself surrender to the demand of his embrace. He laughed softly, moving her against him so that she was more than ever aware of the raw power in his body.

'You *are* afraid,' he taunted, his voice low and husky. 'But not of me. It's yourself you're afraid of—afraid you'll find out there's a real woman somewhere inside that glossy exterior.'

She pushed him away angrily. 'You seem to think you know all about me,' she spat, a sharp edge of sarcasm cutting her voice.

He shook his head. 'Not *all* about you—not yet,' he returned, that wicked smile curving his seductive mouth. 'But I think I'm going to enjoy finding out.'

'Don't be so sure,' she countered, grasping at the vanishing shreds of her composure.

He laughed. 'We'll see,' he murmured, a note in his voice that she could take as a threat or a promise. 'Yes, we'll see.'

He turned and walked on to where he had parked the motorbike. Rachel followed reluctantly. She would have liked to have been able to insist on going home in a taxi instead—she didn't want to get on that bike with him. There was something so...intimate about riding behind him like that, her arms wrapped so closely around his body, totally dependent on him.

But the glint of challenge in his eyes as he held out her crash-helmet had to be defied—she wouldn't give him the satisfaction of being able to taunt her again that she was afraid of him. His smooth technique might be having a damaging effect on her, but he needn't think that all he had to do was snap his fingers...

Flashing him a last withering glare, she pulled on the crash-helmet and swung her leg over the pillion-seat of the bike. He settled in front of her, and she put her arms around him gingerly, trying to keep a small space between them. But as he started the engine and the bike accelerated fast away from the kerb she was forced to hold him tighter.

Maybe it was just because it was dark now, but this time she was much more nervous than before. A tight knot of tension was clenched in the pit of her stomach, but at the same time she was more than ever aware of the hard strength of his body, expertly controlling the bike.

It was no good—she just couldn't fight it. Her breasts were crushed against him, the hot power of the engine was purring through her body. She moaned softly, closing her eyes, surrendering herself to the wanton fantasies that were filling her mind.

The jolt as they turned on to the ramp that led down to the car park beneath their apartment block brought her uncomfortably back to reality. Nick steered the bike smoothly into his parking space, and turned off the engine. Rachel sat back, breathing deeply to try to steady the uncomfortable pounding of her heart.

She was reluctant to take off her crash-helmet, afraid that his perceptive eyes would see in her face the shadow of the dream she had been living. But fortunately the car park was only dimly lit, so she unfastened the strap and lifted it over her head, shaking out her hair as an excuse to avoid his eyes as she handed it back to him.

She walked stiffly over to the lift, his footsteps echoing behind her. That knot of tension was twisting tighter inside her. He must know how vulnerable she was—if he should decide to press home his advantage now, she would be his for the taking.

They didn't speak as they rode up in the lift, but she could sense him watching her, and she drew the thick folds of her ski jacket closer around her throat, as if it were some kind of defensive armour. The lift stopped at her floor, and she stepped out. Then she hesitated, unable to meet his eyes.

'Well, er...goodnight,' she murmured. 'Thank you for a very nice day.'

'My pleasure,' he responded, mimicking her formal politeness.

What was he going to do? Surely he wouldn't let her go without even *trying* to kiss her? Of course, if he made the slightest move towards her...

'What's wrong? Haven't you got your key?'

'Oh... Yes, of course—it's here.' He was leaning one shoulder against the door of the lift so that it wouldn't close, watching her as she fumbled in her handbag. It was a relief when she found the card-key. 'Goodnight,' she repeated, foolishly uncertain.

He lifted one eyebrow in sardonic enquiry. 'Don't I get a goodnight kiss?' he asked.

'Oh, I...have a very busy day tomorrow,' she flustered in panic. 'I always need a good night's sleep when I'm recording——'

'Just one goodnight kiss,' he taunted, catching her wrist and drawing her into his arms. 'I won't disturb your sleep—not tonight.'

She knew she could escape if she wanted to—he was holding her only lightly. But somehow her will had already surrendered. As his head bent over hers, her lips parted to invite his kiss. Their warm breath mingled, and she moved instinctively towards him, reaching up to meet him as his mouth claimed hers. And that sizzling heat had been no illusion—it seemed to scald the delicate membranes of her lips with an unforgettable fire.

His mouth moved over hers, slow and enticing, as the languorous tip of his tongue swirled into the sweetly sensitive corners of her lips. The wild racing of her blood was dizzying her, and she clung to him, wrapping her arms around his neck. He held her close, curving her slender body against the lean, hard length of his, making her deliciously aware of her own vulnerable femininity in contrast to his raw male strength.

A shimmer of response ran through her, and his kiss became deeper and more demanding, plundering ruthlessly into every sweet, secret corner of her mouth. That deep, aching hunger had awoken inside her again, a need so primitive, so powerful that it frightened her. And she could feel the same need in him. A sudden wave of panic gripped her; if she didn't get away from him now, it would be too late—far too late.

He sensed her sudden resistance, and lifted his head, a sardonic glint in his eyes as they gazed down into hers. 'What's wrong?' he enquired, faintly mocking.

'I... Let me go,' she pleaded, gasping for breath.

'Why?'

She tried to push him away, struggling to break his hold on her. 'Let me go,' she demanded, her voice fierce. 'I'll scream.'

He released her so abruptly she almost lost her balance. 'OK—there's no need to get hysterical,' he advised her drily. 'I've no intention of raping you—it isn't my style.'

She stepped back against the wall, her eyes blazing with fury at his cool mockery. 'Go away,' she spat at him. 'Just leave me alone.'

'You sound like Greta Garbo,' he taunted, an inflexion of sardonic humour in his voice. '"I want to be alone." First your ex-fiancé, now me. You'd better be careful—if we both take you at your word, you'll need a hot-water bottle to keep you warm at night.'

She turned sharply away from him, trying hard to concentrate as she fumbled to slip the card-key into the security lock. But as the door clicked open he wrapped his arms around her from behind, drawing her back against him. She was too weak to resist—her bones had melted to jelly.

Her head tipped back against his shoulder, and his hands slid slowly up from her waist to mould the ripe, aching swell of her breasts. He bent his head, sinking his teeth into the side of her neck. She moaned softly, closing her eyes as a tide of pure feminine submissiveness flooded through her. She wanted him, and there was no way she could hide it.

He laughed softly. 'I wonder what you look like first thing in the morning after you've been making love all night?' he murmured, his voice smokily seductive. 'That immaculate hair all tousled, that glossy lipstick smudged with kisses...'

He turned her back against the wall, compelling her to lift her eyes to his. But still she fought, with the last ounce of will-power she possessed, to resist the desire to surrender. If she let him into her apartment tonight, if she let him into her bed, she would be lost. There would be no way she could stop herself falling in love with him.

A wry smile curved his mouth, and shook his head. 'No,' he conceded. 'You're not quite ready yet. Maybe you haven't quite got that creep Chandler out of your system. When I make love to you, I want you to be thinking only about me.'

He put one hand on her shoulder, holding her back against the wall, and then he leaned towards her, his mouth closing over hers. With unhurried ease he sought the secret inner depths, plundering with a flagrant sensuality that took her beyond all reach of reason.

Her body was burning with a fierce desire, and she reached for him, trying to pull him to her, aching for the feel of his strong arms around her again. But he was deliberately frustrating her with his refusal to meet her need. He kissed her long and languorously, and when at last he had taken his fill he lifted his head, his eyes glinting with mocking amusement.

'That was just to be going on with,' he taunted, stepping away from her. 'See you around, princess.'

She drew in a sharp breath between her teeth, red rage filling her head. He had done it again— broken down all her defences, left her helpless with longing, and then let her go. And she had fallen for it a second time. 'You bastard!' she flung at him. 'I hate you.'

His laughter echoed as he swung up the stairs, taking them two at a time.

# CHAPTER SIX

'ARE you all right, Rachel? You look ever so pale.'

'What? Oh... Yes, thank you, Jayne. I...just didn't sleep very well last night.'

'There's a virus going around, you know,' the production assistant warned her with grim relish. 'Once you get it, it's weeks before you feel better.'

'Oh, I don't think I've got that,' Rachel responded quickly, making an effort to pull herself together. Not that particular virus, anyway, though maybe another that had similarly devastating effects. She sat down at her desk, and shuffled through the pile of post that was waiting for her.

'Everything's set for your interview with the Arts Minister this afternoon,' Jayne went on. 'He'll be here at one-thirty, and he must be away by three at the very latest.'

'Fine,' agreed Rachel absently. 'Jayne, didn't I ask you to get me a copy of the financial report on the Royal Shakespeare Company? Really, I asked for it days ago——'

'You asked me on Friday, and it's on your desk,' the girl responded, surprised and indignant. 'There, in the blue folder.'

Damn, what was wrong with her, snapping at Jayne like that? 'Oh, yes ... I'm sorry,' she apologised wryly. 'Thank you very much, Jayne.'

'Oh, that's all right. Listen, I've got some camomile tea—it's really good if you've got a headache. Would you like to try some?'

Rachel smiled, trying to make up for her uncharacteristic show of bad temper. 'That would be very nice,' she agreed warmly.

'Right.' Jayne skipped to her feet, and picked up the electric kettle, but as she darted through the door she collided with someone coming the other way. 'Oops... Oh, I'm sorry, Mr Chandler,' she gasped breathlessly. Her scarlet blush betrayed that she was more than embarrassed at bumping into him. 'I'm just going to fill the kettle—would you like a cup of coffee?'

He smiled down at her indulgently, and glanced across at Rachel. 'No, I won't have one just now, Jayne,' he said. 'I'm only stopping for a moment.'

'Oh ... right.' She hurried out, and he closed the door behind her.

Those brief seconds of his exchange with her production assistant had given Rachel space to be ready to face him. 'Hello, Simon,' she managed, her voice taut.

'Hello.' He laughed, recognising the awkwardness of the situation. 'I've come to apologise for the way I acted on Saturday,' he began, a measure of ironic self-mockery in his tone. 'I was wrong to say you wouldn't succeed in making me jealous—I was very jealous indeed, and that's my only excuse. I suppose it served me right,' he added with a wry smile. 'Now we're even.'

Her eyes evaded his. 'That...wasn't my intention,' she protested awkwardly.

'I know,' he agreed at once. 'You're not that kind of person.' He had moved across to her desk, and perched on the side of it. 'Are you...seeing him?' he enquired, a hint of diffidence in his voice.

'No.' It made her feel uncomfortable to have him looming over her like that, and she pushed her chair back a little from her desk to give herself some space, and forced herself to lift her eyes to meet his. 'But it doesn't make any difference, Simon,' she insisted, determined at last. 'It's over between us. It's no good trying to revive it.'

'I see.' It was evidently costing him some effort to accept the finality of her words with a semblance of calm, but he had never been the sort to let his emotions rule him. He managed a wry smile. 'Well, if that's your decision, I can only say I'm very sad,' he responded in a measured tone. 'I suppose we'll have to come to some arrangement about the apartment?'

'Yes. If you agree, I suggest that I should buy out your half,' she put to him.

'Will you be able to afford that?'

'Oh, yes, I think so. I've done my sums.' He was doing it again, patronising her; as if she would have suggested buying him out if she couldn't afford it!

'Very well. I'll make an appointment with the solicitor,' he said. He rose to his feet. 'I hope...at least we can still be friends?' he asked diffidently.

She smiled up at him, feeling a warmth towards him now that it was all settled. She had really been happy with him, for a while. 'Of course,' she agreed. 'I'd like that.'

There was a tentative tap at the door, and it half opened to reveal Jayne's questioning face. 'The tea's ready,' she offered shyly. 'Can I come in?'

'Of course, Jayne,' Rachel responded, putting on a brisk tone. 'Simon, are you sure you wouldn't like a cup?'

He shook his head. 'No, I've a meeting in five minutes. I'll see you later.' He leaned towards her as if to kiss her, but then seemed to remember, and drew back with a crooked smile. 'Well...' He patted her shoulder instead, and then with a friendly nod to Jayne he was gone.

The girl gazed after him, her young face betraying the unmistakable fact that she had a crush on him. Rachel smiled wryly to herself—half the young girls in the building seemed to feel the same about him. She knew how they had all envied her when she had become engaged to him, and there was probably a good deal of fluttering in the dovecotes now he was free again.

But it was a relief that it was all settled. It hadn't been easy to tell him, but now that she had she was more than ever sure that it had been the right thing to do. It wasn't just because of his affair with Linda. In her heart of hearts she knew that she had never really felt as she ought to...

Like a recurrent fever, the thought of Nick Farlowe flooded into her mind. All night she had lain awake, tossing restlessly, unable to forget the sizzling heat of those kisses; she could feel herself growing warm just from the memory.

But she had work to do this morning, an important interview in a few hours—she had to be fully prepared. She couldn't let herself be distracted. Resolutely shaking her head to dispel the troublesome images, she picked up the blue file and began to read it carefully, scribbling notes in the margin in her neat, flowing script.

She had been expecting that Nick would contact her; probably not on Monday—that would seem too keen. But when Tuesday, and then Wednesday went by with no word, no approach from him, she became puzzled, and then angry. Was he playing some kind of game with her? Did he think that he could ignore her for as long as he chose, and then whenever he snapped his fingers she would come running? Or was he seeing someone else...?

She was constantly on edge—every time she used the lift she was tense in case he should be in it, and she found herself checking his parking space to see if his motorbike was there every time she walked through the basement car park. And she stayed well away from the squash courts.

It disturbed her, the way she couldn't stop thinking about him—it was becoming an obsession. All week she had been fighting the temptation to go down to the cuttings library and see what information they had about him. It was stupid really—didn't she know herself, all too well, how unreliable the stuff they printed in the tabloids could be? But it was no good trying to argue rationally with herself—she was a long way beyond the reach of reason.

With a click she closed her briefcase, and rose to her feet. 'I won't be long, Jayne,' she announced, ultra-cool. 'If anyone calls, tell them I'll ring back.'

The library was on the fourth floor. She felt a foolish twinge of embarrassment as she pushed open the door, as if she were a schoolgirl sneaking to the cloakroom to smoke an illicit cigarette. The senior librarian glanced up with a smile of recognition. 'Ah, yes, Rachel. What can I do for you?' she asked pleasantly.

'I'm . . . looking for some biography on Nicholas Farlowe,' she explained, trying to keep her tone light. 'I'm thinking of doing a piece about art investors—you know, the kind of people who buy the work of up-and-coming young artists, and make a fortune when they become popular.'

She felt herself blushing slightly—why had she bothered to make up that story? No one would trouble to question why she was asking for information about Nicholas Farlowe, even though he had no apparent connection with the scope of her programme.

'Farlowe... Hmm.' The librarian turned to her card index. 'Yes, we should have something on him,' she mused. 'Farlowe, Farlowe...' Rachel waited, trying to look nonchalant. 'Ah, here we are. Hang on, I'll fetch it for you—I won't be a tick.' She dived in among her filing cabinets, and was back a moment later with an orange personality folder. 'Here you are. Do you want to book it out?'

'No, it's all right—I'll just glance through it here,' she responded quickly. She didn't want anyone—especially Simon—to ever see that she'd been interested in the file. She carried it over to one of the desks and sat down, and, drawing a deep breath, she opened it.

It was full of newspaper cuttings. Some were from the financial pages, or from business periodicals, dry stuff about the progress of his various holdings. She put those aside, and picked up the more lurid pieces culled from the pages of various tabloids.

'Playboy Stole My Girl'—some male bimbo complaining that Nick had enticed away his model sweetheart, complete with photographs. She was pretty—blonde, with curly hair and an angel face. She hadn't lasted long. Next was 'Millionaire in Love Triangle'—a model again, and another who called herself an actress, both claiming *they* were his *one true love* and that the other was just a pushy little nobody.

Then there was 'Duke's Daughter Declares I Love Him'. She read that with some interest. There were several articles about it, spanning a period of several months. The first showed a picture of some aristocratic-looking blonde hanging adoringly around his neck, smiling into the camera like the cat who had got the cream. Nick was smiling too, but there was no mistaking the glint of sardonic amusement in his eyes. Indulging his taste for classy birds, Rachel reflected tartly, laying the cutting down on the pile.

The Duke's daughter had proceeded to make a complete idiot of herself over him, causing a scene at Smith's Lawn and almost getting herself drowned at Henley. The last picture was a pathetic one of her sitting on a doorstep—presumably his—in a bedraggled ballgown.

Rachel glanced at the date of the last cutting; it was two years ago. There were no more stories about his private life after that. Either his brush with the clinging débutante had put him off women for a while, or he had managed to avoid the publicity-seeking kind.

She shuffled again through the cuttings, looking long at the photographs of him; those familiar features, that ruffled blond hair—she was almost tempted to steal one of them to keep... Oh, this was getting ridiculous—it was bad enough sneaking in here like a spy, searching out every crumb of information about him.

Tucking the cuttings quickly back in the folder, she returned it to the desk.

'Did you find what you wanted?' enquired the librarian, coming to take the file back from her.

'Oh...yes, thank you. There wasn't a great deal I could use—I may have to think of someone else,' she managed to answer, hoping her voice didn't sound too strange.

'Well, come down again if you need to—we're always happy to help.'

'Yes... Thank you.' She stepped out into the corridor—and almost collided with Simon. 'Oh!' She started guiltily, her face flushing.

He smiled down at her. 'Ah, Rache—there you are. I was hoping I might catch you today.'

'Yes, Simon?'

'What's wrong? Have you been running?' he enquired, concerned at her breathlessness.

'No—I just... It made me jump, bumping into you like that,' she explained quickly. 'What did you want me for?'

'I've made an appointment with the solicitors for Monday, to arrange to sign over the lease. Will that be convenient for you?'

The serious look in his dark eyes brought her down to earth. 'Yes, of course,' she responded. 'What time?'

'Eleven-thirty. And...there was something else,' he added, almost tentatively. 'I wouldn't want you to get the wrong idea, but... Well, I'd got these as a surprise for you, and it seems a shame not to use them. If you'd rather not come, I'll quite understand.'

From his inside pocket he drew two printed tickets, and put them into her hand. Her eyes widened in surprise. 'Tickets for Wimbledon!' she gasped. 'How on earth did you manage to get hold of these?'

He smiled, tapping his finger to the side of his nose. 'Contacts,' was all he would reveal. 'Well? Would you like to come? No strings,' he added quickly as she began to frown. 'I won't read anything into it, I promise. Just good friends?'

She hesitated, sorely tempted. It had always been one of her dreams, to see a Wimbledon final. In her early years in London, she had queued for hours, days, just to catch an odd hour or two of a women's doubles fifth-round match or the semi-final of the All England Plate.

She looked up at him warily. 'All right,' she agreed. 'Just good friends.'

Wimbledon fortnight's legendary curse of bad weather had been escaped this year. The day of the men's singles finals was a glorious English summer day, the sky a flawless blue from early morning. Simon parked his BMW on the car park of the Wimbledon Cricket club, and they walked across the road to the magnificent wrought-iron gates of the All England Lawn Tennis Club.

Today there were virtually no queues—earlier in the week they would have snaked out of sight around the corner. But there were crowds, packing the wide concourse, milling in the public enclosure, surging around the competitors' entrance beneath the ivy-clad walls of the centre court as people craned to catch a glimpse of the star players arriving in their sleek chauffeur-driven cars.

It was like some glorious fashion parade; not quite as formal as Ascot, of course, but still a chance for the women and girls to show off their summer finery. Rachel had chosen a loose cotton dress of glowing pink, and had bound her hair back from her forehead with a twisted silk scarf of the same shade. Simon, like most of the other men, was wearing a light summer suit.

'I think we've time to sample a glass of champagne before we go in,' he suggested, taking her arm.

She glanced up at the clock nestled in the ivy above the members' balcony. 'Oh, no,' she protested. 'It's nearly a quarter to two already. We don't want to miss the start of the match.'

He lifted one faintly quizzical eyebrow. 'It's really hardly worth bothering with the first set,' he argued. 'We can go in when the action starts to warm up a bit.'

Her disappointment showed on her face. 'But I've come to watch the tennis—we can drink champagne any time,' she protested.

He smiled down at her indulgently. 'All right. Come on, then, let's go and get our seats.'

They followed the throng up the long flight of steps, and down into the green well of the Centre

Court. Rachel settled back in her seat, closing her eyes and turning her face up to the sun. 'Mmm,' she sighed contentedly. 'Isn't it lovely and warm?'

Simon laughed, letting his arm rest casually along the back of her seat. 'Glad you decided to come?' he asked. His tone was light enough, but there was a hint of seriousness in his eyes that made her feel vaguely uncomfortable.

'Yes, of course,' she responded, putting on a breezy manner. 'It's a perfect afternoon for tennis. I'm really looking forward to the game.'

Before he could say any more there was a welcome diversion, as the occupants of the Royal Box filed in to take their places—the Princess of Wales and the Duchess of York, both looking cool and relaxed, and of course the Patron of the Lawn Tennis Association, the elegant Duchess of Kent.

The stands were filling up rapidly now, and there was a buzz of excitement in the air. Rachel leaned forward, eager for her first glimpse of the players as they emerged from behind the canvas screen . . . but instead her eye was caught by the gleam of sunlight on a familiar blond head.

Her heart bounced. Why did he have to be *here*? She barely noticed as the two players came out on to the court, though she applauded automatically with everybody else. He must have sensed her gaze, because he glanced over his shoulder and saw her. A faintly mocking smile crossed his handsome face, and she looked away quickly.

The players were warming up, knocking balls backwards and forwards across the net with slow, lazy strokes. The line judges had settled into their chairs, the young ball boys and girls in their uniforms of the traditional Wimbledon colours of sage and purple were up on their toes, ready for their big moment. The umpire leaned forward and spoke into his microphone, his voice booming softly around the enclosed space. 'Two minutes.'

The force that drew her eyes back to him was stronger than gravity itself. He had made some compromise with the semi-formality of the occasion, in that his shirt was plain white, but he had already discarded both his jacket and his tie, and had unfastened his collar and rolled his cuffs back over his strong brown wrists. A slight breeze had ruffled his hair—if indeed it had ever been neatly combed. He was sitting between a middle-aged man and a tall, strikingly attractive woman, and he was leaning close to the man, nodding at something he was saying, but again his eyes lifted to meet Rachel's, and held them captive.

What kind of spell was he weaving now? The crowds, the sunny afternoon, were fading. She was in his arms, her mouth scorched by his kisses, her body aching as he caressed her... She fought to resist the images, but they flooded her brain, possessing her.

The match began, and he turned calmly to watch it, setting her free. She drew a long, steadying breath, fighting to subdue the pounding of her heart. Beside her, Simon seemed completely absorbed in the game, quite unaware that anything was wrong, but though she tried to concentrate all her attention on the action on the court she found her gaze drifting again and again towards that broad back.

She didn't want to be in love with him. Those newspaper cuttings should have been warning enough, if she had needed it—none of his affairs seemed to have lasted very long, and he was always the one to end them. She could feel some sympathy for those silly young girls who had worn their hearts so plainly on their sleeves—it was a pain she could share...

'Forty thirty.'

'Set point,' murmured Simon, close to her ear. 'Good game, isn't it?'

'Oh...yes, it is. Very exciting.' She had to glance up at the score-board to see who was winning.

The defending champion was serving, and he sent over a careful shot, not prepared to take any risks with this crucial point by trying to serve an ace. His opponent sent back a tricky cross-court return, and they were into a fierce rally, fighting to the death.

Every spectator was watching in hushed anticipation, breath held every time the ball crossed the net. The defending champion was at the baseline, powering his shots down, forcing his opponent to chase for every ball, but he hadn't

won yet. A sharp volley, a short ball—he raced
in and just got his racket beneath it. The other
player darted and returned it, but he reached it
at full stretch, placing it with eye-perfect pre-
cision just millimetres inside the line.

'Game and first set . . .'

Rachel joined enthusiastically in the applause.
She wasn't going to allow herself to even glance
along the seats in front of her. The players were
quickly into the second set, their adrenalin fired
up into a fierce competitiveness that had all
twenty thousand people in the audience on the
edge of their seats.

It was a very good match. The fourth set went
to a tie-breaker, and the defending champion finally won by three close sets to two. 'Do you want
to stay and watch the presentation?' Simon asked
as the cheering subsided.

She shook her head. 'No—let's go and get our
strawberries and cream, so we can be back in our
seats for the women's doubles.'

'We'd better try the Park, then,' he suggested.
'It gets so packed in the enclosure down by the
gate that you can hardly move.'

They eased their way out of the crowded stand,
and down the steps at the far end of the centre
court. But there was no escaping the crush—a
steady flood of people was moving along the
paths between the back courts, all heading for
Aorangi Park. Already long queues were forming
at the refreshment booths, and nearly all the
tables were taken.

Simon glanced around, a flicker of impatience crossing his face. 'This really is ridiculous,' he grumbled. 'The place is far too small for a big international event like this. Why don't they do the sensible thing, and move it to somewhere a little more convenient?'

'But then it wouldn't be Wimbledon,' she pointed out with a light laugh. 'It's all part of the tradition—like the rain!'

'Well, it's a good job it hasn't rained this week,' he countered rationally. 'It looks as though we're going to have to sit on the grass.'

'That's OK—it's nice and dry.'

'Wait here, then,' he said. 'There's no point in us both queueing up—I'll bring the dishes over.'

She moved across to a grassy bank raised a little above the trampled path, and settled herself down. All around her groups of people were picnicking from summery hampers, while on the far side of the park, beyond the eating area, were the rows of marquees hired by big commercial companies to offer hospitality to their important business clients.

Rachel eyed them with faint resentment. She knew that the sponsorship they had brought in was vital to the game, but by buying up all the tickets at inflated prices they were keeping the *real* fans out. Oh, no doubt quite a few of those now sipping the chilled champagne and nibbling at the luxurious buffets of smoked salmon and caviare were genuinely interested in the tennis. But for many it was simply a social occasion, something to casually drop into the conversation at their next dinner party, sure to impress— 'Oh, yes, we were at Wimbledon this year...'

'Why the frown, princess?'

She glanced up sharply, catching her breath. Nick had been walking along the path with a group of people whose well-dressed, prosperous air suggested that they were the very kind she had just been mentally deriding. The woman who had been sitting next to him, a striking redhead, had a possessive hand on his arm, but he detached himself with a brief excuse and strolled over to Rachel.

'Oh... Nothing,' she responded quickly. 'It was just the sun in my eyes.'

He laughed, and stretched his lean length lazily on the grass beside her, propping himself up on one elbow and plucking a stem of grass to chew.

'Your... friends are waiting for you,' she pointed out, hearing the note of strain in her own voice.

'Oh, they're just some business acquaintances,' he remarked dismissively.

Maybe so, but that woman was looking back over her shoulder, and if looks could kill Rachel would have been checking her life-insurance policies.

'So what are you doing with Chandler?' he enquired, watching her with that faintly mocking smile that she always found so disconcerting. 'I thought it was all over between you.'

She felt a surge of anger. All week he had ignored her, as if nothing at all had ever happened between them, and yet he had the nerve to question her going out with Simon! 'We're still friends,' she informed him glacially.

'Oh, yes?' There was distilled cynicism in his voice. He reached out and lifted her left hand. 'Still no pretty diamond ring back on your finger, though,' he derided softly. 'What's wrong? Can't quite make up your mind?'

She snatched her hand away as if he had burnt it. 'That's none of your business,' she retorted with a snap.

Those blue-grey eyes glinted knowingly. Very slowly he let his fingers trail down her arm, a touch so light, so tantalising, she could feel the heat of it spreading right through her. 'Just a friendly concern,' he murmured tauntingly. 'I wouldn't want you to make any serious mistakes.'

'I don't think I'm in danger of making any mistakes, thank you,' she managed, trying hard to freeze her responses.

'No? But then you haven't fully explored the alternative yet,' he pointed out, his low, husky voice caressing her.

She knew she shouldn't say it, but he seemed to be hypnotising her, drawing her against her will into his game. 'Wh…What alternative?' she stammered.

'The one I suggested in the first place—chucking him over, and taking up with me instead.' He let his fingers trail back up her arm.

'I think you'll find, once you've been in my bed, that the choice really isn't so difficult to make.'

She stared into his eyes, her breath warm on her lips, her heart racing. He was so right—if she should ever let herself succumb to his practised seduction, she would be lost. Nothing else, no one else, could ever be quite the same...

She started as a shadow fell across them, turning to squint up into the sun. Simon was standing there, two dishes of strawberries and cream in his hands, his face set in an expression of grim fury. 'Oh... I... er, hello, Simon,' she greeted him lamely. 'You remember Nick Farlowe?'

Nick rose easily to his feet, his lazy smile conveying a sardonic amusement in the situation, which Simon clearly did not share. He looked as if he would have liked to hit him, but first he would have to decide what to do with the strawberries and cream.

'Well, enjoy the rest of the tennis, you two,' Nick remarked blandly. 'See you around, princess.' He sauntered away, his hands in his pockets, utterly relaxed.

There was a silence like a four-minute warning. Rachel slanted a wary glance at Simon from beneath her lashes. He was still wearing that frozen expression. 'That damned playboy!' He sat down abruptly on the grass beside her. 'I don't like him hanging around you, pestering you.'

'He... He wasn't pestering me. He just came over to say hello,' she managed to respond.

'Did you know he was going to be here?'

'No, of course I didn't.'

He handed her a dish of strawberries, and she took it without a word. That one brief conversation with Nick had unsettled her to a degree that alarmed her. Just one look from those mocking blue-grey eyes could heat her blood to a fever.

It was crazy—why had she never reacted like that to Simon? Other girls did—young Jayne, her own production assistant, would go visibly weak at the knees whenever he walked into the room. Rachel had always thought it was because she just wasn't the kind—but clearly she was as vulnerable as anyone else when it came to the right man...

The right man? That was a laugh, she reflected with a trace of bitter irony. Nick Farlowe was very much the *wrong* man. Of all the men she could have chosen to fall for, he was the worst. He played at love like a game, quite unscrupulous about who got hurt.

The disembodied voice of the public address system announced that the final of the women's doubles competition was due to start in five minutes. 'Shall we go?' enquired Simon, still tight-lipped.

'Oh... Yes, all right.'

They left their empty dishes on a nearby table, and made their way amid the stream of people back to the centre court.

## CHAPTER SEVEN

THE rest of the day passed without any further encounters with Nick. His party didn't return to their seats until midway through the first set of the women's doubles final, and though Rachel couldn't help but be aware of him, and of the elegant woman beside him, she would not allow herself to look in their direction.

During the break before the last match she and Simon went instead to the smaller enclosure beneath the south wall of the Centre Court, where Fred Perry's statue presided benignly over the crowds. Nick didn't appear there, much to her relief.

It was almost seven-thirty in the evening before the mixed doubles finished. The heat of the day had been eased by a cool breeze, and the hard tension of the earlier matches had given way to a more relaxed, friendly atmosphere, with even some light-hearted banter between the players and the spectators.

As the court finally cleared, the last presentation having been made, Rachel yawned and stretched in her seat. 'Ooh!' she sighed wearily. 'This plastic is very hard to sit on for so long.'

Simon laughed, and offered her his hand to lift her to her feet. 'Come on, let's go,' he suggested, holding on to her hand for a little longer than was strictly necessary.

They made their way for the last time down the steps, and past the high hedge alongside the now empty public enclosure. Just for a fleeting moment Rachel wondered if Nick might be somewhere behind them, if he might see them. Quite deliberately she tucked her hands into Simon's arm.

'I'm so tired,' she remarked by way of explanation as he glanced down at her in surprise. 'It must be all the fresh air. I just want to go home and have nice cool shower, and fall into bed.'

'Oh... I thought perhaps we... might have dinner somewhere?' he suggested, the serious glint in his eyes warning her that he was hoping a romantic evening might begin to change her mind.

She managed to put on some kind of smile. 'Not tonight, Simon,' she responded, trying for a light tone. 'I really am too tired.'

'Very well.' He covered her hands with his. 'I'll take you home.'

She was silent as they walked to the car. The traffic was very heavy, and it took them nearly three quarters of an hour just to reach Merton Road. But after that they were able to turn away from the main stream, and cut through Wandsworth and Clapham, and so via the Elephant and Castle to Tooley Street.

Simon took the big grey BMW up to the kerb, and reaching across took her left hand, stroking

the pad of his thumb gently over her bare fingers.
'I've still got your ring in my pocket, Rache,' he
murmured. 'Any time you want it back where it
belongs, you only have to say the word.'

She hesitated, her mind a whirlpool of confusion. Ever since Nick Farlowe had strolled so
arrogantly into her life, he had turned it upside-
down—if this was love, she wanted no part of it.
Maybe she *should* marry Simon—she needed the
haven of security that he had always seemed to
offer. He might have had that one lapse, but it
was quite out of character...

'I... I need more time, Simon,' she heard
herself respond. 'I can't decide just like that.'

'I don't expect you to. You can have all the
time you want. Just remember one thing—I love
you, I want nothing more than to marry you. I
know I made a bad mistake, but, believe me, I've
learned my lesson.'

He spoke so sincerely that she could no longer
doubt that he was telling the truth. If only her
own emotions weren't in such turmoil—if only
she had never met Nick Farlowe!

Simon leaned across and drew her into his
arms. With a small shock of horror she realised
that he was going to kiss her. It would be the first
time since... His mouth closed over hers, warm
and firm, expecting a response. But there was no
heat—it was just a kiss.

Disappointment, then guilt, then a deep qualm
of misgiving ran through her. Why couldn't she
respond? It had always been all right before...

She curved herself against him, letting her lips part to invite the familiar invasion of his tongue into her mouth. Try, she told herself. Don't think about anything else, anyone else...

At last he lifted his head, and she could tell by the raggedness of his breathing that he had been considerably more aroused than she was. He gazed down at her, his eyes dark with a hungry possessiveness. 'Why don't we ring your mother first thing in the morning, and tell her the wedding's back on?' he suggested softly.

She hesitated, her mind in turmoil. Should she? *Could* she? 'I... Not yet, Simon. Just give me one more night to think about it. I'll give you my answer in the morning. I promise.'

He smiled wryly. 'All right,' he conceded with tolerance. 'Until tomorrow, then.' He drew her towards him for another kiss.

She closed her eyes, trying to let herself relax. She *did* like being kissed by Simon—he was always gentle and considerate. She could be happy with his kisses, and it would be the sort of happiness that could last. Not a fierce, dangerous fire, that would burn itself out in one magnificent conflagration, and leave only ashes.

She smiled up at him as he let her go. 'Goodnight, Simon,' she whispered tremulously. 'I... Goodnight.'

'Goodnight, my darling.'

He squeezed her hand, and she climbed quickly out of the car. Maybe...maybe she ought to invite him to come up the apartment. Maybe if they

were to make love together after all, it would help
her to be sure of her own mind . . .

But as she hesitated, still uncertain, he put the
car in gear and pulled away from the kerb, lifting
one hand in a gesture of farewell. She waved
back, and turned into the brightly lit entrance,
the smile with which she acknowledged the night
porter's greeting just a little too brittle.

She slept badly—how could she expect to sleep,
with such an important decision on her mind?
All night the argument raged inside her head,
back and forth. How could she marry Simon,
when she knew she didn't love him? And yet she
*wanted* to be married to him . . . And love wasn't
absolutely necessary to a successful marriage—
plenty of marriages did very well without it, when
the two partners were so much in tune in other
ways. But when she was in love with someone
else . . . ?

Maybe she should tell Simon the truth about
Nick. It was wrong to deceive him; she ought at
least to give him the chance to make up his own
mind whether he still wanted to marry her. But
how did you find the words to explain that sort
of thing to someone? How did you start?

As dawn paled the sky, she climbed wearily out
of bed, and, wrapping her Japanese cotton
kimono around her body, she padded out to the
living-room. The window drew her over to gaze
at the view. The river looked beautiful at this time
of the morning, the buildings on the far bank

fading blue into the early mist, the peaceful water sheened with pale gold.

How little it had changed, since Claude Monet had painted his picture, over a hundred years before. That picture... Her mind lingered on the memory of what had happened next, of dancing in Nick's arms up there on the roof-garden, with the scent of jasmine drifting around them...

She closed her eyes, clenching her fists with the effort of trying to drive that image from her mind. She had fought so hard against falling in love with him; she really *did* prefer the steady, orderly relationship she had with Simon. Even that one lapse of his didn't really seem to matter all that much any more.

But was that really a good basis for a marriage? another voice inside her head persisted. That she could regard the thought of his being unfaithful to her with such equanimity? And why had it been so easy for her to keep her resolve not to sleep with him before their wedding? Why had she even suggested it?

Because theirs wasn't a physical relationship, she insisted to herself. It was more spiritual...

*Hooey!* You're just making excuses. If Simon could make you feel the way Nick makes you feel, there would have been absolutely no question about it. Well, if you marry him, you won't be able to go on making excuses—you'll *have* to sleep with him. And every time he kisses you, you're going to be remembering the way Nick kissed you...

Impatiently she shook her head, refusing to listen to that treacherous whispering any longer. Maybe a swim would do her good. The pool would be deserted at this time of the morning, and the lure of the cool, clear water was very tempting. Twenty minutes' hard exercise might help to soothe her jangled nerves. Turning back into the bedroom, she slipped off her kimono and reached into the drawer for a swim-suit.

It was a sleek one-piece of shimmering, body-hugging cerise, cut stylishly across one shoulder and high on the thigh. Over the top of it she pulled on a paler pink cotton tracksuit, and slipped her feet into a pair of cork-soled sandals. Then, taking a large towel with her, she let herself out of the apartment and rode down in the lift to the health-club complex in the basement.

The pool area was screened from the lounge by a partial wall of brick, banked with a profusion of leafy plants. The water looked cool and inviting, but as she stepped down on to the tiled surround her footsteps faltered. She wasn't alone.

Someone was powering down the length of the pool—someone with hard, powerful muscles in his shoulders, and blond hair. She took a step back, thinking of retreat, but he had already seen her, and stopped at the side of the pool, levering himself far enough out of the water to rest his folded arms on the edge.

'Hi there, princess,' he greeted her, those blue-grey eyes glinting with mocking amusement as he noticed her hesitation.

'Hello.' Her voice sounded odd to her own ears. Pull yourself together, she warned herself sharply.

His eyes slid over her body, making her acutely aware of every curve beneath the clinging jersey of her tracksuit. She bit her lip, feeling a slow blush spreading up over her cheeks. It was going to be even worse when she had on only her thin swim-suit—and he was making no secret of the fact that he was looking forward to the sight.

'Come on in—the water's lovely,' he invited, his voice husky with anticipation.

'Oh ... Good ...'

She drew a deep, steadying breath. She would have liked to have made some excuse about changing her mind, but to do that would have been to admit that she couldn't control the situation between them. She half turned away from him, and, kicking off her flip-flops, she quickly slid off the lower half of her tracksuit and dropped it on to the terracotta tiles surrounding the pool.

'Mmm—nice legs,' he taunted provocatively.

She spun round to face him, her eyes blazing. 'I've come down here to swim, not to provide you with a free floor-show,' she threw at him.

'I'm sorry,' he responded at once, but there was no trace of apology in his smile, and he had dropped his chin on to his folded arms, watching her, waiting for her to take off the rest of her tracksuit.

And somehow her anger was melting in the heat of his gaze. She felt her heart begin to race a little faster, felt her body grow warm. Slowly, almost as if hypnotised, she pulled at the tracksuit top, lifting it up and stripping it off over her head, aware as she did so of the ripe swell of her breasts against the taut fabric of her swim-suit. She tossed the tracksuit aside, and stood very still.

It was almost as if she were naked—every contour of her body was revealed by the clinging fabric of the swim-suit. A strange quiver of arousal ran through her. He didn't say a word— he didn't have to. The electricity seemed to crackle in the air between them.

She moved to the edge of the pool, feeling his eyes following her as she dived in gracefully. It was a relief to feel the cool water close around her, hiding her, carrying away the heat that had suffused her body. She cleaved through the water, swimming as hard as she could—but he was beside her, pacing his speed to hers. At the end of the pool she turned, and swam back, and then down again, length after length, exhausting herself.

At last she had to stop. Out of breath, her muscles aching, she clung to the rail at the side of the pool. Nick surfaced beside her, very close. Grasping the rail on each side of her, he had effectively trapped her—she didn't have the energy left to evade him.

His body glistened with diamond-drops of water, and she found herself gazing in a kind of awed fascination at the hard, sculpted muscles across his broad chest, at the darkened whorls of blond hair lying against his bronzed skin. That primeval hunger was stirring inside her, and as she lifted her eyes to meet his she knew that he felt it too.

'So where's the boyfriend?' he enquired, an acid edge to his mockery. 'Left him upstairs in bed, have you?'

'No, I haven't,' she countered, her eyes sparking with anger.

'No?' He lifted one quizzical eyebrow. 'You mean you didn't let him stay the night?'

'No, I did not!'

He laughed, that low, husky laugh that could turn her bones to jelly. 'That's good,' he murmured, his eyes hungrily possessive as they gazed down at her. 'I was jealous.'

That admission startled her. 'J...jealous?' she repeated weakly.

'That's right. The thought of him with you, doing the things that I want to be doing with you...' He drew himself closer against her, until their bodies were almost touching. 'Tell me something,' he demanded, his voice rough-edged. 'Do you look at him the way you look at me? When he kisses you, do you melt inside the way you do with me?'

She stared up at him, struggling desperately to fight the weakness he engendered inside her. She wanted him, as much as he wanted her. It was a feeling that frightened her, a feeling that was alien to her whole character—or so she had always believed. 'I . . . I don't know what you mean,' she stammered, unable to escape the hypnotic compulsion of his gaze.

His eyes glinted with a dangerous light. 'Don't you?' he murmured tauntingly. 'Then perhaps I'd better remind you.'

She didn't even try to evade him as his head bent over hers—she knew that she could only surrender to a temptation that had become irresistible. The tip of his tongue flickered into the sensitive corners of her lips, and then swept languorously deep inside, finding all the sweetest, most sensitive parts of her mouth.

That now familiar heat sizzled through her. What chemical reaction between them could cause such fire? He was curving her back against the side of the pool, and as she felt the brush of his hard male body against hers a lurch of excitement caught at her heart. She reached up and wrapped her arms tightly around his neck, clinging to him, out of her depth, as he kissed her with a fierce possessiveness, as if seeking to obliterate the memory of any other man from her mind.

All the wild desire that had been growing inside her for the past two weeks surfaced irresistibly, and communicated itself with wanton clarity to the man who was holding her so tightly. He lifted his head, and his eyes blazed down into hers.

'I want you, princess,' he growled. 'And don't try to pretend that you don't feel the same, because your body tells me everything I need to know.'

Very deliberately he wound the thick hank of her wet hair into his fingers, drawing her head back so that she was curved against him with an intimacy that flamed her blood to white heat. She gazed up at him, betrayed by a weakness as old as Eve. She had forgotten where she was, and as his caressing hand stroked up to mould the aching swell of her breast she knew that the instant ripening of her nipple revealed to him all her response.

He laughed softly, his thumb brushing across the tender bud, and a shimmer of hot pleasure rippled through her. She closed her eyes, melting helplessly into a languorous sensuality. She did not even protest as he slid the narrow strap of her swim-suit from her shoulder, drawing the clinging wet fabric slowly down to uncover the warm swell of her naked breasts.

She moaned softly as she felt the brush of his fingers over her bare skin. His lips were dusting scalding kisses across her face and down into the sensitive hollows of her throat, as with magical skill he teased the taut, ripe bud of her nipple, reducing her to a state of total abandon.

He had lured her far beyond the realms of rational thought. Nothing seemed to matter except the exquisite pleasure of this moment. She moved against him instinctively, helpless in the grip of some fierce elemental force that was beyond all her power to control. His mouth returned to claim hers again in a kiss that demanded all she had to give, his body was crushing hers against the side of the pool, making her devastatingly aware of the fierce tension of male arousal in him.

'*Now* try and deny it,' he challenged fiercely. 'You want me.'

Her head fell dizzily back, and a small, husky sob escaped her impeded throat. She couldn't deny it . . . But as her eyes flickered open she realised with a stab of horror where they were. She strained against him, trying to push him away.

He laughed, low in his throat, subduing her struggles with ease. 'Have you ever made love in a swimming-pool?' he taunted, a glint of evil intent in his eyes. 'I've never done it before, but I'm always ready to try something new.'

Sheer panic gave her the strength to break free of him. She backed away from him, appalled by the thought of what she had almost allowed him to do to her. The flicker of sardonic amusement in his eyes as they drifted down over her reminded her that the top of her swim-suit was still down to her waist, and she tugged it up quickly to cover herself, her cheeks scarlet with humiliation.

How could he have made her behave like that? What if someone had come down and caught them? She would never have been able to hold her head up again. Desperately she looked around for the ladder out of the water, holding up her swim-suit with one hand.

His mocking laughter followed her as she fled to the lift, pausing only to snatch up her tracksuit and towel. He was sitting on the side of the pool, watching her in amusement, like some clever predator, content to bide his time. The downlights in the roof glowed on his bronzed skin, defining those hard muscles, making him look like some perfect, sculpted statue.

The lift seemed to take an eternity to arrive. She wrapped herself up in her towel—she had dropped one of her sandals, but she wasn't going to go back for it. As soon as the lift doors opened she darted into it, pressing the button urgently for the fourth floor. The little pool of drips she was leaving on the carpet caused her a twinge of guilt, but that would quickly dry out and disappear. Her self-respect would not be restored so easily.

A hot flush of shame suffused her cheeks. She had given him every reason to believe that she would comply with his outrageous demand. In another few moments he would have stripped her swim-suit off completely, would have curved her naked body beneath his...

*No.* She shook her head, desperately trying to dispel the vivid image from her mind, but it wouldn't leave her alone. Her body ached, unfulfilled, and she could see the taunting triumph in his eyes as he claimed his victory... A single tear trickled from the corner of her eye, and traced a slow path down her cheek.

With relief she let herself into the flat, and closed the door behind her, leaning against it, her eyes closed. She needed a shower—she needed to cool the simmering heat in her blood. Quickly she crossed to the bathroom, and, peeling off the wet swim-suit, she stepped under the sharp, ice-cold needles of water, gasping as they stung her skin.

It was like a penance. She stayed under the shower for as long as she could stand it, and then towelled herself briskly dry. But she felt better for it, her head clearer than it had been for some time. Wrapping herself up in her kimono again, she walked back into the bedroom, and, sliding open one of the mirrored doors that concealed the capacious wardrobes, she pulled out one special hanger, unwrapping the garment-bag and laying out the contents on the bed. Her wedding dress.

Actually it was a suit—more appropriate for a civil ceremony than some romantic, flowing gown. It was of smooth ivory crêpe de Chine, the jacket embroidered with tiny seed-pearls, and to go with it was a chic little pillbox hat with a neat veil to cover her eyes. Rather a conservative outfit, perhaps, but it had a certain style—just the sort of thing that Simon would approve of. And her mother.

She sat down on the bed, gazing at the suit. It seemed to represent what was safe and familiar—Simon, and the well-ordered future they had planned together. They were going to live here in

London for a few years, but at some time they would buy a place in the country as well. And then they would have children—just one or two, as both their parents had had. Not a large, boisterous family—that wouldn't fit in with the sort of lifestyle they had envisaged at all.

But she couldn't marry Simon now—of that at least she was finally certain. She was in love with Nick; the touch of his hands on her body had branded her, and she could never belong to anyone else.

Restlessly she rose to her feet, and paced over to the window, and stood gazing out. A small eddy was bubbling in the current, drifting down the river with the tide. As she watched it pass her window, and disappear in the shadows under the arch of Tower Bridge, her mind drifted with it.

When she was young, she had dreamed of getting married in a church. She would have worn the loveliest dress, all antique lace, and she would have had three or four little bridesmaids in dainty white dresses, with bright summer flowers in their hair...

Wryly she shook her head. Probably every young girl had those dreams at one time or another. But she was past thirty, not some dewy-eyed teenager. Romantic dreams were a waste of time—to indulge in them would only bring her more pain. Because Nick only wanted her for a casual moment—he had made it more than clear that he wasn't ready to make any kind of commitment.

* * *

It wasn't easy to tell Simon. At first she was tempted to take the coward's way, and call him on the telephone, but at last she managed to convince herself that she must face him in person. In fact he took the news quite well—better than she had expected—but she still wasn't absolutely sure that he had accepted that this was her final decision.

She spent the evening trying to work—not with any great deal of success. She just couldn't concentrate on anything—her mind was filled with thoughts of Nick, and nothing she could do would banish them. Restlessly she rose to her feet, and paced over to the window.

The river was flowing timelessly between its banks, dark and tranquil amid the bright hurly-burly lights of London. It had a romantic magic that was all its own—that magic that had surrounded her the evening she had danced with Nick, out on his roof-garden, with the fragrance of honeysuckle in the air and the low, sensuous notes of a saxophone drifting around them...

A rap on the door startled her, and she looked round. Who, at this time of night...? And without passing the security desk? She hesitated, her heart pounding. She knew who it was. She wouldn't open the door—he would get the message, and go away eventually...

But some compelling force, stronger than all her powers to resist, was drawing her across the room. Her hand was trembling as she reached out to open the door. He was leaning his shoulder casually against the frame of the door, and the way he let those blue-grey eyes rake down over her body made her mouth feel suddenly dry.

'Like Cinderella, you left this behind when you ran away from me this morning,' he said, holding out her sandal. 'And like Prince Charming, I'm bringing it back.'

'Oh...' She took it from him, knowing that she should just thank him and then make some excuse to close the door. But she couldn't—it seemed that none of her actions was under her own control.

'Is Chandler here?' he enquired, glancing past her into the apartment.

'No.' The admission was surprised out of her, but, of course, he didn't know that she had finished with Simon completely—thank goodness; that was her one means of defence.

He smiled in lazy mockery. 'Poor guy. You do keep him on short rations, don't you?' he remarked, moving slightly towards her and forcing her into retreat.

'Our relationship... isn't based on that sort of thing,' she countered, tilting her chin at a haughty angle.

'Isn't it? Then what is it based on?'

'Oh... on mutual liking, and respect. And... Oh, I really wouldn't expect you to understand.'

'Try me.'

'Oh, we share the same tastes,' she responded with dignity. 'We like the same music, the same plays. We can talk about poetry...'

He laughed with sardonic humour. 'Well, there I concede he's got one up on me. I only know one poem, and I wouldn't sully your dainty ears with it. And as for music—well, my tastes are more Springsteen than Shostakovich.'

'I like Bruce Springsteen too.'

'Ah, well, then—we have something in common after all.' He had moved closer to her again, and she took another step back. Now he was right inside the apartment. 'But, for all his catalogue of virtues, you're not going to marry him,' he asserted with confidence.

She couldn't retreat any further—her knees seemed to have turned to jelly, and she had to lean back weakly against the wall. But she lifted her eyes defiantly to his, determined not to succumb to the mesmerising power in his gaze. 'Aren't I?' she countered. 'What makes you so sure?'

'Because you're not in love with him.' He brushed the backs of his fingers lightly over her cheek, sending a sizzle of electricity right through her. 'You're in love with me.'

She caught her breath as his head bent over hers. That familiar heat swirled in her blood as their lips met, dizzying her, and she had to put up one hand to his chest to steady herself. Her fingertips encountered the hard wall of his chest, and she was lost. Her lips parted in unconditional surrender. She belonged to him—he had won the game, and the spoils of victory were his.

## CHAPTER EIGHT

NICK'S kiss was warm and enticing, his sensuous tongue swirling languorously over the delicate inner membranes of Rachel's lips, exploring with unhurried ease to find all the sweetest places. His arms had wrapped around her, curving her slender body intimately against his hard length, making her vividly aware of just how much he wanted her. She clung to him, responding with a hunger as urgent as his own, her blood heated to fever pitch, her body aflame with desire.

He lifted his head, his eyes burning with a hungry possessiveness as they gazed down into hers. 'I want to make love to you, Rachel,' he murmured, a husky note of insistence in his voice.

'Yes,' she whispered, unable to refuse him anything. He had used her own name. She loved the way he called her princess, but to hear him use her own name, so intimately...

He smiled with satisfaction, and, scooping her up in his arms, he carried her across the room to the bedroom, as easily as if she weighed no more than a feather. He laid her down on the bed, and she reached up for him, drawing him to her, her mind a giddying whirlpool of desire.

Her hair had begun to slip from the neat chignon she had arranged it in, and with a lilt of soft laughter he pulled out the rest of the pins and ran his fingers through the long, silken strands, spilling them across the pillow. 'What's happened to the stuck-up bitch I met a fortnight ago?' he taunted. 'Can this be the same woman?'

No—she would never be the same woman. It was a frightening thought, but it was too late to change her mind about this now—far too late...

His mouth returned to claim hers again, demanding all she had to give, and she responded without restraint, offering him her heart, her body, all she had. He lifted his head, smiling at her eager willingness, and then with rapt concentration he began to unfasten the tiny pearl buttons down the front of her silk blouse, one by one.

A delicious tension of anticipation was rising inside her. He was taking his time, lingering luxuriously over every beautiful moment, weaving a magic that was luring her into a land of sensuous experience that she had never visited before.

Slowly he stroked the soft fabric aside, and his eyes glowed with a simmering desire as he gazed down at the warm swell of her breasts hiding in the delicate lacy cups of her bra. He breathed a deep sigh, burying his face in the soft valley between. 'You're so lovely,' he murmured, almost reverently.

She curled her fingers into the crisp hair at the nape of his neck, curving her body invitingly beneath him. His jaw felt hard and rough against her silken skin, but she didn't mind—she revelled in the contrast between his raw maleness and her soft femininity.

He lifted her in his arms, easing her blouse back off her shoulders and tossing it aside, and then with deft skill disposed of her bra. She shivered with heat as she felt the brush of his body against her naked breasts. She had never felt so exquisitely vulnerable, so miraculously powerful.

His mouth closed over hers again in a kiss of pure possession, long and deep, plundering every sweet corner of her mouth, and she yielded totally, a languid tide of pleasure flowing through her whole body, melting her bones. And then he began to caress her, his hands moving over her body, slowly, but with an unmistakable intent that made her quiver with delicious anticipation, until at last he cupped one aching breast in his long, clever fingers.

The delicate pink nipple was the focus of a million sensitive nerve-endings, responding with searing intensity to the teasing brush of his thumb. Her head tipped back into the crook of his arm, and she heard the sound of her own breathing, harsh and impeded, the sound of her own pulse pounding in her ears.

His kisses were scorching hot, tracing a path of fire over her trembling eyelids, across her delicate temple, and into the shimmeringly sensitive hollow behind her ear. She moaned softly, tortured by pleasure, curving herself against him invitingly. But now that he had her, he was taking his own time, so that her need burned inside her like a fever.

It was as though he knew her every response, finding with unerring skill every sensitive spot and arousing her to an almost unbearable peak, and then moving on, luring her deeper and deeper into his own world of erotic pleasure. She followed blindly, almost frightened by the power of her own primeval hunger.

His kisses moved on, down the long, vulnerable curve of her throat, dusting her smooth shoulders with flame. And then at last he reached the ripe swell of her breasts, and her spine curled in ecstasy as she felt the hot, rough lap of his tongue over one tender nipple, swirling it as if it were a ripe, succulent fruit for him to savour and devour, drawing it deep into his mouth to suckle with a rhythm that pulsed right through her.

She was drowning in the most exquisite sensations, her body shimmering with the magic he was weaving around it. Never in all her most vivid dreams had she imagined that anything could be like this—and yet she had seen the promise of it in his eyes, the very first time he had looked at her.

His hand dropped to the hem of her skirt, lifting it back over her thighs, to find that she had a preference for wearing stockings and suspenders. He lifted himself on one elbow to admire the picture she offered, half-naked, her skirt up around her waist, only a tiny pair of white lace briefs to cover her modesty. She peeped up at him, shy, and he laughed teasingly.

'Mmm—that's just what I like,' he growled huskily, smoothing his hand up over her silk-clad thigh and playfully snapping one suspender.

'Hey,' she protested, pretending to be angry. 'Don't do that.'

'So take them off,' he suggested.

She drew a long, steadying breath, and climbed off the bed. Her fingers were clumsy, fumbling with the clasp of her skirt, but at last she managed to unfasten it and draw down the zip, stepping out of it and folding it carefully over the back of a wicker chair that stood by the bed.

He was watching her, the lust in his eyes flaming her blood. Emboldened, she let a small, provocative smile play around the corners of her mouth, and, perching herself gracefully on the edge of the chair, she slowly unfastened one suspender, rolling down the silk stocking inch by inch.

He laughed softly, appreciating the private floor-show. She took off the other stocking in the same way as the first. Now she was wearing only the dainty white lace briefs, and the shim-

mering string of pearls that circled her throat.
He held out his hand to her.

'Come here and lie down,' he coaxed.

She took his hand, her heart pounding so hard
he could surely hear it.

He drew her down beside him, and smoothed
his hand down over her naked body in a possessive gesture. 'A real classy bird,' he murmured smokily.

She put up her hand, and stroked her finger-
tips lightly along the hard line of his jaw, fascinated by the slight rasp of his skin. 'I love you,'
she whispered, her whole heart in her words.

He bent over her, his eyes smiling. 'Good,' he
asserted with satisfaction.

She reached up to him, folding her arms
around his neck to draw him down to her, her
lips parting hungrily to welcome his kiss. His
weight was crushing her into the bed, but she
didn't mind. A tide of pure feminine submissiveness was flooding through her, a primitive instinct, as old as Eve.

Laughing with triumphant pleasure, he knelt
up, astride her stomach, and she gazed up at him,
breathless as she watched him pull his T-shirt up
over his head and toss it carelessly on to the floor.
The sheer masculine power of his body was
beautiful. Hard muscles moved smoothly beneath bronzed skin, lightly scattered with curling
blond hair, and the subtle musky scent that was
exclusively his own rose to drug her senses.

He came back into her arms, the brush of naked flesh against naked flesh inflaming them both. His hands were caressing her with slow, warm sensuality, and their mouths broke reluctantly apart to draw a ragged breath. His hot tongue began to explore the delicate shell of her ear, tracing tiny circles in the sensitive hollow behind, until she moaned with the sheer pleasure of it, her body curved against his in wanton invitation.

The touch of his hands was magical, arousing every inch of her, and she caressed him in return, thrilling to the latent strength of the hard muscles in his back, challenging the danger of a primeval male arousal that was barely held in check. Their bodies entwined, exchanging pleasure for pleasure, hungry kisses tasting the sweetness of each other's flesh.

All her defences, all the inhibitions that had once held her prisoner, had long since crumbled into dust. As he gazed down at her, his eyes lingering over every soft curve of her body, her heart thrilled to the hungry intent she sensed in him.

She was naked except for her tiny briefs. The wispy scrap of white lace was hardly any covering, the soft triangle of down that crowned her thighs showing like a shadow beneath it. But the significance of removing it shimmered in the air between them. It was the last barrier...

His eyes held hers, reassuring her with his promise of gentleness, but a tremor of vulnerability ran through her as he eased his fingers beneath the lace and drew it slowly down over her slender hips. He bent his head, and placed one kiss at the very top of her thigh. And then inch by inch he drew the wispy thing down, his kisses following, down to her slim ankles, her dainty toes.

She half closed her eyes, stretching in languorous sensuality like a kitten. He laughed huskily, drawing her back into his arms. 'Mmm— the things I want to do to you,' he murmured, low in his throat.

'Such as?' she invited, half shy, half bold.

'Such as this.'

His hand slid down to coax apart her thighs. A shimmer of submission ran through her, but she trusted him implicitly, yielding to the gentle touch of his fingers as he sought the most intimate caresses. A slow, warm melting had begun, deep in the pit of her stomach, as he found the hidden seed-pearl of desire, arousing it with such infinite skill that she sobbed with pleasure.

'And then this.'

He bent his head to the same place, and as the sinuous tip of his tongue swirled languorously over that tiny nub of sensitivity hidden deep within its velvet fold she lay back on the pillow, the fires inside her raging out of control.

And at last he moved to lie above her, ready to demand the ultimate surrender. With one gentle hand he brushed the hair back from her face, kissing the corners of her eyes. 'I love you, Rachel,' he murmured smokily. 'I love you.'

A wave of the most incredible happiness flooded through her, and she offered her body willingly to his hard possession, a gasp of mingled pleasure and shock breaking from her lips as he took her. She wrapped her arms around him, moving with him as the deep, driving rhythm mounted. Some elemental force had taken control of them both, swirling them through the rapids, drowning them in whirlpools of fire. The sweet intensity seemed almost too much to bear, yet still it gripped her, fiercer and hotter, like a tide of molten gold, bearing her up on wave after wave of sheer ecstasy.

This was what she had waited for, for so long— this one perfect moment of eternity. The man whose sweat-slicked body she held in her arms was the one she loved, and she belonged to him now, totally and irrevocably. And at last with a sobbing cry she felt herself swept over the edge of sanity, clinging to him as with a final tumultuous surge he fell into her arms, his heart thundering next to hers.

They slept for a while, and then woke together, their minds in tune, their bodies already hungry for each other again. They made love all through the night, and as dawn broke they fell asleep again, replete, tangled up in each other's arms.

It was full morning when Rachel finally woke. Nick was still asleep, one arm flung possessively over her body, his dark lashes shadowing his cheeks, his breathing deep and slow. She gazed at him, scarcely able to believe the happiness that filled her heart. He had said he loved her.

But even as she lay there, close beside him in the bed still warm and rumpled from their love-making, the first shadows of doubt began to taunt the fringes of her mind. He had only said it while he was making love to her. Could such a fragile love survive the bright light of day?

She turned her head to gaze around the room. It was a beautiful morning—the golden sunlight filtering through the windows bathed the gleaming wood floor, highlighting the patterns of veining in the pale beech.

Into her heart treacherous voices were whispering, and she found herself remembering the things she had read in those newspaper cuttings. She fought to push them aside—didn't she know, only too well, how scurrilous those gutter journalists could be?

And yet . . . what guarantee did she have that this affair would last longer than even this one night? None at all. Though he had said he loved her, for all she knew he might say that to every woman he made love to. He had made no promises, no commitments. He could just walk away and leave her—today, tomorrow, next year...leave her with nothing but the ashes of her dreams.

Frightened by her own vulnerability, she sought instinctive refuge within the brittle defensive shell of her composure. The first thing she had to do was get out of bed, get her clothes on—then maybe she might be able to begin to think straight.

Cautiously she lifted his arm from across her body, and tried to ease herself out from beneath it. But he opened one eye, the gleam of mocking amusement in it telling her that he hadn't been asleep for some time. 'Where do you think you're going?' he teased.

'I...I want to get dressed,' she responded, struggling for the resolve to arm herself against him.

'Why?' He drew her close, so that she could feel the warm strength of his hard male body against hers, stirring the embers of arousal in them both. 'Mornings are the best time, you know.'

He let his hand stroke down slowly over her soft, naked flesh, caressing. But she stiffened, fiercely suppressing her response. 'Don't!'

He lifted one eyebrow, startled by her venom. 'What's wrong?'

'I...want to talk.' She moved out of his arms, and he let her go. Her cotton kimono was on a hook behind the door, and she picked it up, wrapping it around her body and tying the belt

in a secure knot. But she was acutely conscious
of him watching her.

'Is it absolutely necessary to get dressed in
order to talk?' he enquired, an inflexion of sardonic humour in his voice.

'Yes, I think it is,' she responded, donning as
much dignity as she could muster.

'Ah!' There was a world of cynicism in that
one syllable. It didn't augur well for what she
wanted to say. He had hoisted himself up against
the pillows, folding his hands comfortably behind
his head, his lazy smile hinting that, though she
might be fully covered now, he was still seeing
her as she had been last night, naked and flushed
with lovemaking. 'OK,' he said. 'I'm listening.'

How could she begin? She hadn't rehearsed it,
and with him looking at her like that... 'I just...I
don't want this to be just a one-night stand,' she
blurted out.

'Nor do I.'

'No, but...I don't want it to be just a casual
affair.' Oh, but his body was so beautiful. Those
hard muscles across his chest... She just wanted
to be held there, to let his warmth infuse her, to
breath the musky perfume of his skin...

'So what *do* you want?' he enquired baldly.

'I want to get married.' There—she had said
it. All she could hear was the pounding of her
own heartbeat as she waited for his answer. The
glint of mockery that had appeared in his eyes

warned her that it wasn't going to be the one she wanted to hear.

'I see,' he responded drily.

She drew a deep, steadying breath. 'Last night you ... you said you loved me,' she pursued, clenching her hands at her sides to stop them trembling.

'Yes ... ?'

'Did you ... did you mean it?' she pleaded.

'Yes, I did. But I don't remember proposing marriage.'

A horrible giddiness was dragging at her, as if she were riding backwards on a down-bound escalator. But pride held her stiffly erect. 'What's wrong with getting married?' she demanded, tilting up her chin.

'Oh, I've nothing against it,' he drawled, coolly indifferent. 'I'm sure it's an excellent institution.'

'Well, then?'

He shrugged his shoulders, dismissing the subject. 'If I ever decide to get around to it, I'll do it in my own good time.'

She could feel the tears stinging the backs of her eyes, but she blinked them back fiercely. She would *not* cry, at least not in front of him. 'I see. Well, that's clear enough. At least I know where I stand.' She picked up his clothes, which were scattered all over the floor, and tossed them on to the bed. 'In that case, would you please leave?'

He lifted one eyebrow in sardonic enquiry. 'You're telling me that unless I marry you, it's all over between us?'

'Yes, it is,' she insisted resolutely, though her heart was close to breaking. 'I'm not prepared to sit around and wait—maybe forever. I'm thirty-one years old—I want to be married.'

'Well, if you feel that way, maybe you'd better take up Chandler's offer after all,' he suggested bluntly, swinging out of bed and pulling on his jeans.

She stared at him, stunned with pain. How could he tell her to marry Simon, after what had happened between them last night? But if that was how much he cared about her... 'Maybe I will,' she retorted angrily.

His eyes hardened. 'You're really so desperate to get a ring on your finger that you'd marry a man you know you're not in love with?'

'Why shouldn't I?' she countered, chilled by his contempt. 'At least he's not afraid of a *serious* relationship!'

'Then I wish you happiness,' he responded with shattering indifference, and, picking up the rest of his clothes, he walked out of the apartment.

The closing of the door broke the last remnants of her self-control. She collapsed on to the bed—the bed that still bore the lingering musky scent of his skin—and let herself cry. She had known—she only had herself to blame. He had never pretended that he was offering any more than he was prepared to give. He had made it plain from the start that he wasn't the permanent kind.

She cried until she was exhausted, her eyes sore and her throat aching. If she had cherished any last hope that he might relent, might call her on the phone or come down to her door, it had finally gone. She had to accept that, though he might have said he loved her, he wasn't prepared to follow that through with any kind of commitment.

So what did she have left now? Nothing— nothing but the ashes of her dreams. At least she didn't have to face the studio today; rolling on to her back, she laughed at the bitter irony of that. Her programme was off the air now, until the start of the new autumn schedules, and in the break she had been going to get married. Today she had planned to go up to her parents' home in Alderley Edge, to get ready for the wedding.

Well, she would go anyway; she couldn't stay here, not with Nick so close—she would go mad. She needed the peace of that big, comfortable red-brick house, with its large, leafy garden. And even if her mother would probably nag, her father would understand.

'I hope you don't expect me to have any sympathy for you. If you hadn't been so foolish and capricious, passing up a nice young man like Simon... Well, it's none of my business, I suppose. I just hope you won't come to regret it, once it's too late.'

'Leave the lass alone, Betty. She's been home three days, and you've done nothing but carp at her.'

Elizabeth Haston favoured her husband with one of her scornful looks. 'It's all very well for you, but I had to face Alicia Wardle-Cooper at the bridge club last night. Her *youngest* has just got engaged—to an investment consultant—and she's only nineteen! Really, the way she goes on, anyone would think it was going to be another Royal Wedding.'

'Rachel doesn't have to get married just to give you something to boast about to that silly Wardle woman.'

'Did I say she did?' his wife countered, drawing herself up indignantly. 'Of all the nonsense. But I *did* like Simon—so presentable, and such excellent manners.'

Her father caught Rachel's eye, and grinned with wry humour. '*And* he was having a bit on the side,' he reminded his wife mischievously.

'Don't be crude,' she snapped, and stalked away before she was in danger of losing the argument.

Rachel sighed, smiling at her father. 'I'm afraid I'll never convince Mum,' she said. 'So far as she's concerned, Simon was the bee's knees.'

He looked at her, his eyes shrewd. 'So long as you're really sure yourself?' he enquired with gentle concern.

'Oh, yes, I'm sure.' She smiled, maybe a little crookedly. 'It wasn't just...because of his affair. In a way, that was a good thing—it made me realise something I had never really admitted to myself before. I couldn't have been happy married to him. He...he sort of took me over— as if I were just an extension of himself, not a person in my own right at all.'

'Well, you were right not to marry him, then,' he assured her, nodding in understanding. 'Just between you and me, I won't say I'm sorry. I always thought he was a bit of a stuffed shirt.'

She looked at him in surprise. 'Did you, Dad? You never said.'

'Nay, but I wouldn't, would I? He was your choice. And besides, as you said, your mother thought the sun shone out of his backside.' His eyes glinted with amusement at having been proved right. He rarely argued with his wife—he just bided his time, and in the end he usually got his own way.

Rachel kicked off her shoes, and tucked her feet up beneath her. They were sitting on the sunny terrace at the back of the house, having just finished dinner. The garden was filled with the fragrance of roses, drifting on the warm evening air.

The sweet perfume evoked the memory of that afternoon in her apartment, the afternoon she had first met Nick. Her father sipped his tea, watching her with shrewd eyes—he knew she wanted to confide something, but just as when she was a child he was prepared to wait patiently until she was ready to spit it out.

'But that wasn't the main reason either,' she began, gazing at her toes. 'There was...this other man, you see. I met him the day I first split up with Simon—maybe that was why it all happened.'

Her father nodded, his kind eyes filled with sympathy.

'He was completely the opposite of Simon.' She laughed unsteadily. 'He rides a motorbike. And he's younger than me—oh, not by much, but he's too young to want to settle down.'

He lifted one enquiring eyebrow. 'If you only met him the day you split with Simon, you can't have known him very long,' he pointed out.

'No, but...it wasn't the kind of relationship that was ever going to develop slowly,' she explained with care.

Her father smiled understandingly. 'I think I know what you mean.' He nodded. 'It was pretty much the same between me and your mother.'

'Was it?' She regarded him with interest. It wasn't something she had ever really given much thought to, although she knew that her parents hadn't known each other very long before they had got married.

'So what's happened to this young man?' he asked.

She smiled wryly. 'I wanted to get married, and he didn't, so...'

'Maybe you were just rushing him a little,' he suggested gently. 'If a man thinks a woman's only interested in getting a ring on her finger, he isn't very likely to respond.'

She shook her head. 'I couldn't just have an affair with him. How would I know how long it would last?'

'Do you think getting married would give you any sort of guarantee?' he countered.

'Well, no, but...Dad, are you actually *telling* me to have an affair with him?'

'I'm just telling you to follow your heart. Respectability isn't everything, you know—though for goodness' sake don't tell your mother I said so!'

'Maybe you're right...' she mused thoughtfully. 'Yes!' Her eyes began to dance, and she bent and kissed him quickly on the cheek. 'Thanks, Dad—I'm going to go up and pack right now!'

'Leave me to explain it to your mother,' he said. 'Don't worry, I'll bring her round.'

She smiled gratefully. 'She'll throw a purple fit——'

'Trevor, there's a motorcycle in the drive.'

Rachel turned quickly as her mother appeared at the french windows again; by her expression she had clearly taken it as a personal affront that one of the alien horde had dared to trespass on her well-tended gravel.

Her father slanted her a questioning glance. 'Could this be your young man?'

'Maybe...'

'Who do you know that rides a motorcycle?' her mother demanded, shocked.

'If it's who I think it is, you'll find out soon enough,' Trevor advised her, taking her hand to prevent her following Rachel out into the hall.

Rachel's heart was pounding in trepidation as she walked to the front door. *Was* it him? She hardly dared open the door...

Those blue-grey eyes smiled down into hers. 'Hi, princess.'

'Nick!' She didn't even wait to hear why he had come—she threw herself straight into his arms, tears of happiness streaming down her face.

He caught her up, kissing her long and lingeringly, a kiss that demanded total possession, and she gave it all, holding nothing back. 'Well, if I'd known I was going to get a reception like that, I'd have come days ago!' He laughed as at last he lifted his head.

'I was just going to pack. I was coming back tonight.'

He raised one enquiring eyebrow. 'Back to me?'

'Yes. If you still want me. On your terms,' she promised breathlessly.

He smiled slowly. 'So—you finally got your priorities sorted out?' he asked, a teasing glint in his eyes.

'Yes. I couldn't marry Simon— I'd already told him that, before... before...' Her cheeks tinged pink at the delicious memory.

'I know. As soon as I found out, I rang your sister-in-law to get your address—fortunately there aren't too many Hastons in the phone book, so it didn't take me too long to find her. I think you and I have a few things to discuss,' he added seriously.

She was gazing at him, puzzled. 'But... how did you know I'd decided not to marry Simon?' she asked.

He frowned, then said gently, 'Haven't you heard? I'm sorry—I thought you must know about it already.'

'Know about what?'

Slowly he drew the London evening paper out of the front of his leather jacket, and gave it to her. It was open at an inside page, and her own photograph smiled up at her—it must have been a library one, at least six months old. 'New Autumn Schedules' ran the headline.

'I don't believe it...' She read the story in growing horror.

'In a controversial decision the popular Arts programme *In Review* has been axed. A spokesman for the studio, Mr Simon Chandler, said this morning, ''We have decided to aim at the youth market, with an entirely new format. Naturally we are very sorry to see Miss Haston go.'' Rachel Haston, 31, was formerly engaged to Mr Chandler, executive producer. She was not available for comment today.'

'I don't believe it! I'm under contract... There wasn't even an inkling of this last week.'

'It looks as if your Simon can be a very swift mover when he chooses.'

'Of all the mean, spiteful things to do! I never thought he could be so petty-minded. Well, if they want to get rid of me, I shall make them pay through the nose for it! They needn't think I'm going to take this lying down. I've a damned good mind to go straight to the opposition—or, even better, set up my own production company and make them come to me for programmes!'

He hugged her, sweeping her right up off her feet. 'Good for you!' he encouraged enthusiastically. 'You'll be brilliant at it.'

She laughed happily, but her eyes held a wry expression. 'I don't know,' she demurred. 'I'm all right in front of the cameras, but I've never had any production experience, let alone dealt with the business side.'

'You've been in television for five years,' he argued. 'You must have picked up a good deal in that time.'

'Yes, I suppose so...'

'And as for the administration side, all you need to do is hire a good accountant. Someone who knows the business. You must have contacts?'

'Yes. In fact...I think I know someone who might be interested.'

'Well, there you are, then,' he concluded confidently. 'Go for it.'

'Do you really think I should?'

'Of course,' he asserted.

She smiled up at him, wrapping her arms around his neck. 'Maybe I could, at that,' she mused. 'You make me feel as if I could do anything.'

He laughed, and kissed her again. 'And I'll tell you what—if you want to get your revenge on Chandler, I'll buy you the studios for a wedding present, and you can sack him.'

'A...a wedding present?' she repeated, stunned. 'But...you said you didn't want to marry me.'

He shook his head, smiling down at her. 'I never said I didn't *want* to,' he pointed out, a teasing lilt of humour in his voice. 'I've known...oh, maybe from the first moment I saw you in that lift that you were the girl I wanted to marry. But even so I wasn't about to accept your ultimatum the other morning—no one blackmails me.'

'Would you really have let me marry Simon?' she asked.

'I don't know.' His eyes glinted wickedly. 'Maybe I'd have rung him up and told him where you spent Monday night.'

'Oh…' She blushed scarlet. 'He wouldn't have liked that.'

'I don't suppose he would. I didn't like it much when I thought you were spending nights with him.'

She lifted her eyes to his. 'I wasn't, you know,' she whispered. 'I never——'

'I know.' He held her close, burying his face in her hair. 'I'm glad. I wouldn't have expected you to be a virgin—it came as quite a surprise. After all, I haven't exactly lived like a monk myself. But past history was one thing—imagining it still going on was almost enough to make me contemplate murder.'

Happiness was bubbling inside her, bringing tears of joy to her eyes, and he kissed them away gently.

'Come and meet my parents,' she asked shyly.

She took his hand, and led him through to the back of the house. Her mother was sitting bolt upright on one of the wicker chairs, thin-lipped, but her father came forward at once, offering his hand.

'Dad, I'd like you to meet Nick——'

'Farlowe! Of course—I recognised you at once.' He pumped the younger man's hand enthusiastically. 'That was a very shrewd move you made on H.T. Zinc. Must have netted you a tidy profit.'

'It didn't do too badly,' conceded Nick with a grin.

'Well, well. So what's going on?' he added, a hopeful glint in his eyes as he surveyed the two of them.

'May I have your permission to marry your daughter, sir?'

'Of course! I couldn't be more delighted!' He hardly needed to say so—it was obvious from his broad smile.

'Trevor! You surely aren't going to permit your daughter to marry this...this...?' his wife demanded furiously, regarding Nick's red leather motorbike gear with horror.

Trevor chuckled with laughter. 'Well, now, if I recall correctly, she *is* thirty-one years old, or thereabouts. I think she's old enough to know her own mind.'

'Well, you needn't think *I'm* going to approve,' Elizabeth asserted haughtily. 'When I think of poor, dear Simon... And what Alicia will say I don't know!'

## EPILOGUE

'HAPPY?'

Rachel sighed, and smiled up into Nick's eyes. 'Happiest,' she confirmed. 'The happiest of anyone, any time, anywhere.'

'Good.'

She was dancing in his arms, on a golden summer afternoon, beneath the huge red-and-white marquee erected in her parents' garden. A warm breeze stirred in the long veil of antique lace she was wearing in her hair, and close beside her Big Jim Bradley's five-year-old daughter, duskily pretty in her white bridesmaid's dress, with bright summer flowers in her hair, was dancing with Maggie's and Richard's four-year-old son, trying to persuade him to waltz with her like a proper ballroom dancer.

Rachel laughed softly, still scarcely able to believe that all this was true. 'It's incredible,' she breathed. 'Just look at my mother, dancing with Sandro. A month ago she said she wasn't even going to come to the wedding!'

'Ah, it was all just a bit of a shock for her, that's all,' Nick responded, smiling. 'She was bound to come round in the end.'

182

'Not necessarily—you don't know my mother,' she argued. 'She's not like your friends. She cares more about what the neighbours will think than anything else.'

He shook his head. 'Not really,' he said. 'She does care about you—she's just not the kind of person who finds it easy to show her feelings.'

Rachel smiled up at him. 'You're amazing. You've made friends with both my parents, and what's more you've made them friends with each other—better friends than I can remember them being for a long time.'

He chuckled with laughter, a wicked glint in his eyes as he hugged her intimately close. 'Ah, well, you see, since my side of the family doesn't have the resources to come up with much in the way of grandparents for our children, I wanted your side to be perfect,' he explained rationally.

She blushed, lowering her lashes to veil her eyes. 'We did agree to wait until next year,' she reminded him demurely. 'I've a brand-new production company to run—it's going to take a lot of hard work.'

'Mmm—but having a baby wouldn't stop you doing that,' he pointed out. 'Lots of women combine motherhood with a career.'

'I know,' she conceded, trying to argue against her own deepest longings. 'But this is a big challenge for me—I don't even know if I'm up to it yet.'

'Of course you are,' he assured her lovingly. 'You can do anything you want to do.'

She smiled up at him. He gave her such confidence in herself that even the greatest obstacle seemed to evaporate from her path. 'I suppose... Maybe by about Christmas...' she mused.

'Good. I don't want to waste too much time.' His smile was blandly innocent. 'I want at least eleven children.'

*'Eleven?'*

'Yes. Enough for a football team.'

She slanted him a look of speculative enquiry. 'I suppose you wouldn't be prepared to settle for five-a-side?' she asked.

He roared with laughter. 'All right—we'll compromise,' he agreed.

She rested her cheek contentedly against her new husband's broad shoulder. A big, boisterous family—just what she had always wanted. And her new production company was already off to a brilliant start, with an agreement for a documentary on the Glyndebourne Festival Opera, and a series of half-hour programmes on modern dance.

Of course, once they started having babies she would probably only want to work part time, but she had been able to recruit a good team, and the agreed settlement from the studio for the termination of her contract had put the company on a sound financial footing.

'What are you thinking?' asked Nick, smiling down at her.

'Oh, just being quietly amazed at how totally happy I am,' she sighed. 'Just two months ago, I thought I had my future all mapped out. If someone had told me then that today I'd be marrying some gorgeous, handsome blue-eyed guy who rode a motorbike, whom I'd be absolutely crazy about, I'd never have believed them.'

'I'm glad you had a change of heart,' he teased.

'So am I. I must have been mad to think I could be happy with Simon. I do wish him well, though, in spite of that dirty trick he pulled at the end—after all, even that turned out well for me.' A tiny frown ruffled her brow. 'I just hope Jayne will be all right with him. I couldn't believe it when I heard they'd rushed off and got married like that. Of course, she's had a crush on him for ages, but I can't help wondering how she'll feel after she's lived with him for a few months.'

'You leave them to worry about themselves,' he advised. 'I'm just relieved that he's half the world away from you.'

'Oh, I'm sure he'll be a great success in America. It was really lucky for him, being offered that job out of the blue...' Something in Nick's eyes made her look at him sharply. '*You* didn't happen to have anything to do with that, did you?' she challenged.

He conceded a grin. 'Oh, I just made a few calls to some people I know in California.'

She slanted him a questioning glance. 'But why?' she asked, puzzled. 'You don't even like him.'

'I feel safer,' he admitted, holding her possessively close. 'After all, you used to think you were in love with him.'

'Think,' she reiterated firmly. 'That was before I knew what the real thing was like.'

He smiled down at her, moving her to the slow, sensuous rhythm of the music. 'And now?' he asked, a soft huskiness in his voice.

She reached up and wrapped her arms tightly around his neck, her whole body curved against his. 'Now,' she whispered, 'I know.'

# Fall in love with

# *Harlequin Superromance*®

**Passionate.**
Love that strikes like lightning. Drama that will touch your heart.

**Provocative.**
As new and exciting as today's headlines.

**Poignant.**
Stories of men and women like you. People who affirm the values of loving, caring and commitment in today's complex world.

At 300 pages, Superromance novels will give you even more hours of enjoyment.

Look for four new titles every month.

*Harlequin Superromance*
*"Books that will make you laugh and cry."*

# A Christmas tradition...

**Imagine spending Christmas in New Orleans with a blind stranger and his aged guide dog—when you're supposed to be there on your honeymoon!**
**#3163 Every Kind of Heaven**
**by Bethany Campbell**

**Imagine spending Christmas with a man you once "married"—in a mock ceremony at the age of eight!**
**#3166 The Forgetful Bride**
**by Debbie Macomber**

*Available in December 1991, wherever Harlequin books are sold.*

RXM

# HARLEQUIN

## Romance

**This December, travel to
Northport, Massachusetts,
with Harlequin Romance
FIRST CLASS title #3164,
A TOUCH OF FORGIVENESS
by Emma Goldrick**

Folks in Northport called Kitty the meanest woman in town,
but she couldn't forget how they had duped her brother and
exploited her family's land. It was hard to be mean, though,
when Joel Carmody was around—his calm, good humor
made Kitty feel like a new woman. Nevertheless, a Carmody
was a Carmody, and the name meant money and power to
the townspeople.... Could Kitty really trust Joel, or was he
like all the rest?

# "INDULGE A LITTLE" SWEEPSTAKES

## HERE'S HOW THE SWEEPSTAKES WORKS

### NO PURCHASE NECESSARY

To enter each drawing, complete the appropriate Official Entry Form or a 3" by 5" index card by hand-printing your name, address and phone number and the trip destination that the entry is being submitted for (i.e., Walt Disney World Vacation Drawing, etc.) and mailing it to: Indulge '91 Subscribers-Only Sweepstakes, P.O. Box 1397, Buffalo, New York 14269-1397.

No responsibility is assumed for lost, late or misdirected mail. Entries must be sent separately with first class postage affixed, and be received by: 9/30/91 for the Walt Disney World Vacation Drawing, 10/31/91 for the Alaskan Cruise Drawing and 11/30/91 for the Hawaiian Vacation Drawing. Sweepstakes is open to residents of the U.S. and Canada, 21 years of age or older as of 11/7/91.

For complete rules, send a self-addressed, stamped (WA residents need not affix return postage) envelope to: Indulge '91 Subscribers-Only Sweepstakes Rules, P.O. Box 4005, Blair, NE 68009.

© 1991 HARLEQUIN ENTERPRISES LTD.                    DIR-RL

---

# "INDULGE A LITTLE" SWEEPSTAKES

## HERE'S HOW THE SWEEPSTAKES WORKS

### NO PURCHASE NECESSARY

To enter each drawing, complete the appropriate Official Entry Form or a 3" by 5" index card by hand-printing your name, address and phone number and the trip destination that the entry is being submitted for (i.e., Walt Disney World Vacation Drawing, etc.) and mailing it to: Indulge '91 Subscribers-Only Sweepstakes, P.O. Box 1397, Buffalo, New York 14269-1397.

No responsibility is assumed for lost, late or misdirected mail. Entries must be sent separately with first class postage affixed, and be received by: 9/30/91 for the Walt Disney World Vacation Drawing, 10/31/91 for the Alaskan Cruise Drawing and 11/30/91 for the Hawaiian Vacation Drawing. Sweepstakes is open to residents of the U.S. and Canada, 21 years of age or older as of 11/7/91.

For complete rules, send a self-addressed, stamped (WA residents need not affix return postage) envelope to: Indulge '91 Subscribers-Only Sweepstakes Rules, P.O. Box 4005, Blair, NE 68009.

© 1991 HARLEQUIN ENTERPRISES LTD.                    DIR-RL

## INDULGE A LITTLE—WIN A LOT!

# Summer of '91 Subscribers-Only Sweepstakes

## OFFICIAL ENTRY FORM

This entry must be received by: Oct. 31, 1991
This month's winner will be notified by: Nov. 7, 1991
Trip must be taken between: May 27, 1992—Sept. 9, 1992
(depending on sailing schedule)

**YES,** I want to win the Alaska Cruise vacation for two. I understand the prize includes round-trip airfare, one-week cruise including private cabin, all meals and pocket money as revealed on the "wallet" scratch-off card.

Name _____

Address_____ Apt. _____

City _____

State/Prov. _____ Zip/Postal Code _____

Daytime phone number _____
(Area Code)

Return entries with invoice in envelope provided. Each book in this shipment has two entry coupons—and the more coupons you enter, the better your chances of winning!

© 1991 HARLEQUIN ENTERPRISES LTD.                    2N-CPS

---

## INDULGE A LITTLE—WIN A LOT!

# Summer of '91 Subscribers-Only Sweepstakes

## OFFICIAL ENTRY FORM

This entry must be received by: Oct. 31, 1991
This month's winner will be notified by: Nov. 7, 1991
Trip must be taken between: May 27, 1992—Sept. 9, 1992
(depending on sailing schedule)

**YES,** I want to win the Alaska Cruise vacation for two. I understand the prize includes round-trip airfare, one-week cruise including private cabin, all meals and pocket money as revealed on the "wallet" scratch-off card.

Name _____

Address_____ Apt. _____

City _____

State/Prov. _____ Zip/Postal Code _____

Daytime phone number _____
(Area Code)

Return entries with invoice in envelope provided. Each book in this shipment has two entry coupons—and the more coupons you enter, the better your chances of winning!

© 1991 HARLEQUIN ENTERPRISES LTD.                    2N-CPS